“I’m curious.”

Morgan continued smoothly, “How far did you intend to go with this substitution? To the altar, or beyond…? Had you intended to slip that tantalizing body between my sheets?”

“My sisterly loyalty doesn’t extend that far,” Rosie replied. “But,” she cried recklessly, “if any man deserves to be left at the altar, you do!”

KIM LAWRENCE lives on a farm in rural Anglesey, Wales. She runs two miles daily and finds this an excellent opportunity to unwind and seek inspiration for her writing! It also helps her keep up with her husband, two active sons and the various stray animals that have adopted them. Always a fanatical consumer of fiction, she is now equally enthusiastic about writing. She loves a happy ending!

Look out for more Kim Lawrence titles coming soon in Harlequin Presents.

A Wife of Convenience

KIM LAWRENCE

THE MARRIAGE CONTRACT

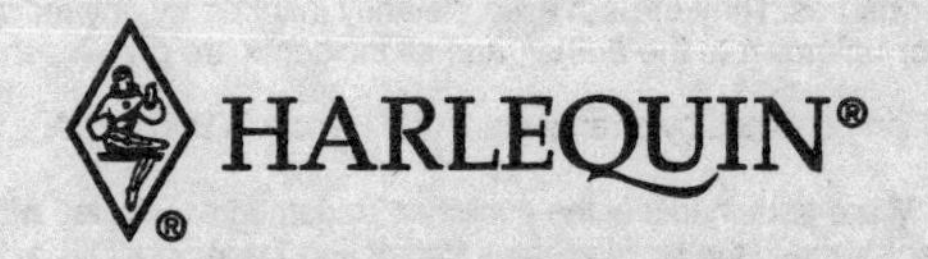

TORONTO • NEW YORK • LONDON
AMSTERDAM • PARIS • SYDNEY • HAMBURG
STOCKHOLM • ATHENS • TOKYO • MILAN • MADRID
PRAGUE • WARSAW • BUDAPEST • AUCKLAND

ISBN 0-373-80537-3

A WIFE OF CONVENIENCE

First North American Publication 2003.

This edition published by arrangement with Harlequin Books S.A.

Visit us at www.eHarlequin.com

Printed In U.S.A.

CHAPTER ONE

THE LIBRARY was no euphemism for a couple of bookshelves, Rosie realised, examining the impressive book-lined room. This room, like the whole house, spoke of affluence. With a knowledgeable glance she considered the paintings that were hung on the oak-panelled wall; they showed an eclectic taste and unrestricted funds.

Now that the butler had withdrawn she took the opportunity to acquaint herself thoroughly with her surroundings, surroundings which she was presumably meant to be familiar with. She felt as if 'guilt' was emblazoned in neon letters across her forehead. The bland expression of the sober-suited individual who had ushered her in had been interpreted by her feverish brain as suspicion.

Logic told her that was foolish; though her twin was half an inch taller, and she was slightly more generously endowed across the bosom, nobody, not even their parents had ever been able to tell them apart. Vague disapproval, she told herself, was probably a prerequisite for a butler.

Even last night the idea had never seemed likely to succeed, but now turning tail and running was an impulse difficult to withstand. If only she'd had the determination to stand firm against Elizabeth's pleading, but her twin had employed a nice mixture of moral blackmail and charm—not that being able to identify the fact in retrospect did her any good, Rosie told herself wryly. If the situation had been different, who knew? It might have been her and not Elizabeth who needed extricating.

Reasons apart she had found herself agreeing, against her better judgement, to become a very reluctant participant in this ridiculous charade. Pretend to be her sister for a few days…had that ever sounded a reasonable proposition? she found herself wondering.

To find out, almost accidentally, that her twin had got herself engaged in a typically whirlwind fashion had been a shock, but to find she had every intention of marrying a man other than her fiancé was mind-numbing, even taking her twin's rather tempestuous lifestyle into account! Being brought up separately meant they had never traded places as children in the mischievous manner she knew other identical twins often indulged in…she'd often felt wistful about this and about much of their childhoods…

But this? This request was something far less innocent. A worried frown knitted her smooth brow as her hands clenched spasmodically.

It would help her, she thought fretfully, to have some clue to the character of the man she was supposed to be marrying, rather than the sketchy details her twin had given her, details she felt sure were bound to be the tiniest bit biased. Elizabeth had made Morgan Urquart sound a distinctly dubious character, almost sinister, she recalled, her ferocious frown deepening at the recollection. She placed trembling fingers over her stomach, which was twisted in painful knots of nervous tension.

'Why, Lizzie, did you agree to marry him, then?' she had asked at the time. Had it only been yesterday? Her twin's eyes, identical to her own—amber, widely spaced and slightly slanted, giving the delicately boned face an exotic look—had widened to their fullest extent.

'Why, Rosie, it seemed a good idea at the time.'

And the mixture of exasperation and affection Rosie always felt in her sister's presence had see-sawed towards the former.

'Don't look disapproving, Rosie. You had to be there. I

was at the most boring party and he just walked in...I mean, you should have seen the women there; every one of them was willing him to look at her—and he looked at me,' she said simply with a sigh. 'He can be so charming when he wants to be and at first I actually thought he was smitten. It was very flattering.'

The red-painted fingernails tapping on the tabletop were an indication of her tension as she recollected, 'Things snowballed after that. Daddy had worked himself into a frenzy thinking about all the goodwill that being related to Morgan Urquart would bring him, and Bill was giving me the cold shoulder, poor lamb. He had this stupid idea he wasn't wealthy enough for me.

'I thought it might bring him to his senses if I got engaged, and Morgan needed a wife because of this weird proviso in his grandfather's will. It wasn't as if he really was smitten, you see.' She had sounded almost wistful at this point.

'It seems an extremely *bad* idea to get engaged to a man you hardly know when you are in love with another.' Her sister's frivolous outlook on life so precisely mirrored their mother's that Rosie could hardly feel surprised at these revelations. 'I don't suppose you gave Bill reason to doubt your fidelity?' she had observed drily. Elizabeth's sighing appreciation of Morgan Urquart had made Rosie wonder whether her twin was being totally honest when she insisted she felt nothing for him.

'Bill isn't like any of the others, Rosie...truly,' Elizabeth had said earnestly. 'I made it clear to him that the idea of waiting for him to earn his first million before marrying me was not a plan I was exactly thrilled by. Bill can be so infuriatingly old-fashioned and noble,' she had observed with an explosion of pride. 'I thought getting engaged to Morgan would make him so jealous he'd forget all those antiquated principles.'

'It appears to have worked,' Rosie had commented.

Elizabeth's droll smile had been tinged with a desperation Rosie had never seen before. 'The problem being Morgan.'

'To put it bluntly, Elizabeth, dump him.' Privately she had thought Elizabeth had acted disgracefully, but there seemed little point in mentioning the fact.

For some reason her twin had found this response incredibly funny...hysterically so. 'You don't understand, Rosie; you've never met Morgan.' The sigh that had shaken her had wrung at Rosie's heart. 'Two days out of your life; that's all I'm asking, Rosie. It means everything to me. Maybe I'm wrong, maybe Morgan would shrug off being dumped, but why take risks when it's my future...Bill's future? If anything happened to him because of me I'd never forgive myself. It's just a precaution.'

Rosie had felt little sympathy with this melodramatic statement. 'For heaven's sake, Elizabeth, the man's hardly likely to take pot-shots at Bill or put out a contract on him.'

'I'd expect something more subtle than that but equally deadly,' her twin had responded mysteriously. 'He doesn't even have to know you're not me; just string him along and do the awful deed when I'm clear of the chaos.' Her tone had suggested that Rosie was being incredibly unreasonable not to happily co-operate.

The guilt she felt increased now as she went over her sister's peculiar reasoning. Whichever way you looked at it she was deliberately fooling a man whose only crime as far as she could see was asking her sister to marry him. A clean, honest break was the course of action she had pleaded with Elizabeth to take. It seemed pointlessly vindictive to let Morgan Urquart nurse false hopes any longer than was necessary. Elizabeth could never have loved him and be so callous, she decided. And am I any better? she thought miserably. Reluctance doesn't equate with innocence.

The poor man would probably be so devastated at being

jilted that he'd have no thought of the fearful reprisal which Elizabeth was convinced he would inflict upon her and her intended husband. The whole thing seemed incredibly elaborate and excessive, but Elizabeth wouldn't be satisfied with less.

Safely married to her Bill and with the Atlantic Ocean between them was the only way, apparently, she would feel safe, and with Rosie's help she had every intention of achieving this. I'll never carry it off, Rosie thought despairingly. But what alternative did she have? Let her twin down, or deceive some innocent stranger. On the other hand, if he was half as awful as Elizabeth had implied he was a long way from innocent!

The sound of raised voices interrupted her distracted thoughts, and the noise of breaking glass and the definite female shriek made her stifle a cry of alarm.

Her instinctive reaction was to go to the aid of the person in distress. She let out a snort of vexation as her heels—Elizabeth's heels; elegant, but not designed for speed—made her stumble over one of the vibrant rugs which were strewn over the marble floor. Caution told her at this point that she should retrace her footsteps, but the fresh sound of weeping made her set her jaw and continue in the direction it emanated from. Her entrance went unnoticed by the two occupants of the elegant drawing room.

Thoughts of rape receded as the young woman dressed in the expensive but unexpected evening gown—it was only ten a.m.—rose with fluid grace from a kneeling position at the feet of the tall man and plastered her scantily clad body against his.

'But Morgan, darling, I know you love me. I'm not too young!' The youthful voice rose to a crescendo. 'If you must marry, why not marry me instead of that stupid creature?'

'Calm down, Ellie.' The man caught the two clinging hands and untwined them from his neck. 'This marriage is by way of being a business arrangement, as you are well aware. Girls who marry at seventeen usually live to regret it, sweetheart, especially when their husbands are thirty-five.'

'Everyone expects you to marry me!' The voice rose to a shrill vibrato that made Rosie wince. 'If your grandfather had waited to die I'd be old enough and you wouldn't marrying that social-climbing slut.'

'I'm sure the old man would have held on if he'd knov what an inconvenience it would be to you, darling.' I turned his head at that point and Rosie became aware th his words were accompanied by a wry, almost indulge smile. She became aware of a lot of other things too!

Her breath froze in her throat. Her sister had said he w good-looking, but she hadn't been prepared for this! F some reason she recalled a carving of a medieval knig she'd seen in an old church as a child: the same long, a gular face, all sharp angles and shadows, and eyes that h haunted her dreams.

These eyes were not dead wood but very much alive grey, pale like river water running over pebbles, alert, intelligent and, as they met her riveted gaze, coldly derisory. Whatever emotion he felt at this scene being witnessed by his fiancée it was neither embarrassment nor remorse, she realised, and she experienced a hot flare of indignation on her sister's behalf. Some of the sympathy she'd been nursing for this man evaporated; it was impossible to equate victim with the individual she was staring at. And she'd heard him with her own ears refer to his marriage as a business arrangement.

'I am popular this morning.' The smile that curved the sensually sculpted lips held neither warmth nor the wry humour she had glimpsed moments before, but his eyes moved over her body—clad in Elizabeth's expensive figure-hugging clothes—with an expression that made her stomach muscles clench in protest.

'I'm intruding…' Only a brief flare of anger betrayed her distaste at the intimate inspection. The outline of his disciplined but sensual mouth drew her eyes like a magnet. It was incredibly expressive.

'True.' One eloquent eyebrow shot skywards as she flushed and lowered her eyes. Elizabeth was never known to blush, she reminded herself, feeling uneasily certain that those penetrating eyes missed very little.

'You!' The girl twisted around, her voice carrying the throbbing note of melodrama that made Rosie certain she was relishing her role as tragedy queen, even though the emotions she radiated were perfectly sincere. The face was pretty in a chocolate-box sort of way, still retaining the round contours of youth. She shook back a mane of fair hair and glared at Rosie through tear-reddened eyes; mascara ran in dark streaks down an over-made-up face. 'I hate you!'

She advanced a step and Rosie interpreted the intent on the stormy face too late. The slap snapped her head sideways and brought tears of pain to her eyes.

'Ellie, you will apologise to my fiancée.' His eyes were remorselessly hard as he enunciated each word with grim deliberation. 'Immediately! You are behaving like a spoilt, over-indulged brat, and,' he added pointedly, 'you look absurd in that get-up. I suggest you go and wash your face; it looks like a hallowe'en mask.' The nicely understated sarcasm was aimed to devastate the over-sensitive teenager and Rosie could see it had succeeded in doing just that.

'I hate you both and I'd die rather than apologise!' The sexy walk she had rehearsed earlier was discarded as she ran headlong from the room.

'That was extremely brutal,' Rosie observed critically. Despite the stinging pain on the left side of her face she could recall the intensity of adolescent emotions clearly enough to feel extremely sorry for the girl, who must by now want to die from sheer humiliation.

'But effective.'

Rosie's lips pursed in disapproval at this heartless sentiment. 'You could have been gentler.' She started violently as a hand touched the burning side of her face, thumb beneath the angle of her jaw and fingers pushing into her hairline.

'Considering Ellie was far from gentle I'm surprised you'd settle for anything less than blood,' he said reflectively. The slight pressure exerted by his fingers forced her to look up into his face; his eyes were on her hair. Against his fingers it shone like black silk, and had a similar texture as it slid across his skin. The permanent furrow between his dark brows deepened fractionally before his eyes met hers.

He couldn't know, she told herself, quelling an instinct that made her want to follow the example of the young girl...what had he called her—Ellie? Was she supposed to know her? she wondered, realising just how many pitfalls there were in her twin's plan and how stupid she had been to succumb to her beseeching plea. The idea she had scoffed at—of this man taking drastic steps when Elizabeth dumped him—no longer seemed quite so melodramatic...there was something dangerous about him.

It wasn't just his indisputable physical presence that troubled her—because he certainly radiated a very sensual, uncompromisingly masculine aura—it was what she glimpsed behind the urbanity and expensive tailoring: a ruthlessness that was disturbingly primitive in its intensity. The butterfly spasms in the pit of her belly grew worse as she suffered the enigmatic stare once more.

'We were all young once.' She tried Elizabeth's high-pitched giggle, the one that sounded so attractive on her sister's tongue, but it emerged like a strangled croak.

'And was that so long ago?'

His voice had a velvety texture, all bitter chocolate. Too rich for her simple palate, she found herself thinking as his voice glided over her sensory nerve-endings, raising goose bumps over her flesh.

'I had no idea your taste ran to schoolgirls, Morgan.' She relaxed a little, immersing herself in the sort of dialogue that was second nature to her sister. If Elizabeth's descriptions of him had been accurate his taste was less than discriminating, she recalled scornfully. He was probably just the sort of heartless womaniser who deserved to be taught a lesson, she reminded herself grimly. As Elizabeth had woefully listed his exploits, the portrait she had drawn in Rosie's mind—of a man without a scrap of moral decency—had made Rosie's toes curl in disgust.

'I'd hardly be marrying you if it did, would I?' he countered, one dark brow arching sardonically. His chin came up and the dark gold hair fell backwards, just touching the dark collar of his jacket.

For some reason Rosie had mentally pictured him as dark; his colouring, like almost everything else, had come as a shock. 'I'm not that old,' she replied archly. Inside she cringed at the fatuous flirtatiousness of her tone.

'And you were never that young, were you?' The voice held a heavy irony and his hand fell away from her face, much to Rosie's relief.

She was puzzled by the way the casual contact repelled her so fiercely; she was well accustomed to people who displayed their emotions with casual tactile warmth. There was no warmth in this man, though. A faint frown played over her face as she raised her head to examine the now austere features.

'We were all that young, though possibly not that uninhibited,' she said slowly, uneasy at the way her scrutiny was being returned.

'The way I hear it you could be particularly, and often publicly, uninhibited.'

Think Elizabeth, she told herself, angry at this blatant slip. Her sister's exploits had been lovingly recorded by the

Press since her teens. 'Poor kiddy, did you perhaps lead her on just a touch?' she purred sweetly. 'She seemed quite convinced that her deep and abiding passion was returned.'

He gave a snort of humourless laughter and moved away with a feral grace she found strangely riveting…the unfulfilled artist in my soul, she told herself as he reached the tall Adam fireplace. He turned back to face her and Rosie shuddered at the coldness in his regard. What had possessed her twin to commit herself to this creature? He was not a man to play games with; that much was obvious at first glance.

'I hope I don't detect jealousy in your voice.'

Under normal circumstances, this wasn't something that a man destined to walk down the aisle in a few days would say to his bride-to-be; but then these were not normal circumstances! 'I'll try and restrain myself,' she assured him gravely, and he looked sharply at her innocent face.

'I'd appreciate that.' An extremely alert expression had drifted into the clear yet conversely obscure depths of his eyes. 'You seem in quite an…unusual mood this morning, my dear.'

'I'm not your dear.' Her eyes sparked with a clear defiance that was all Rosie. He had an edge of patronising condescension that made her spine stiffen. It was probably easier to use casual endearments than recall the names of all the females he slept with, she thought scornfully. According to Elizabeth, his reputation as a womaniser was legendary!

She'd been deluding herself when she'd imagined this man must be in love with her sister; he was as cold as ice. She'd imagined that Elizabeth had overemphasised the convenient nature of this engagement just to excuse her own behaviour. Silently she apologised to her twin. Marriage should mean more than mutual convenience; even she, with a less than favourable attitude to the institution, felt that strongly.

Her own parents' brief and from all accounts totally disastrous union had done nothing to recommend the institution to her. A strong sexual attraction had drawn two people together, two people with nothing in common except the daughters they had produced. And those daughters, rather like the spoils of war, had been divided—one living with each parent.

Rosie had been part of the entourage that followed her mother around the world from one glamorous watering spot to another. Part of the reason her parents had parted had been her father's inability to cope with the burgeoning success of his artist wife, who not only didn't avoid the limelight but positively courted it, admiration being as necessary for her sustenance as oxygen.

Until she had gone to school Rosie had naïvely imagined that all five-years-olds ordered their supper from Room Service.

Her extrovert counterpart, on the other hand, had been reared by strict nannies and a mostly absent banker father. She'd been sent to a school, from which, despite several close shaves, she hadn't been expelled. A conventional upbringing had produced an elegant bohemian; a bizarre lifestyle an exemplary citizen. The irony of this had appealed to Rosie's dry appreciation of the absurd when they had eventually met, like strangers, at eighteen.

When Rosie had chosen to seek out her twin she had half expected to meet a kindred spirit, someone who instinctively knew how she felt. Within five minutes of being in her twin's company she had reluctantly discarded that fantasy; her mirror image had very little in common with her. In fact in many ways they were opposites, but, like many opposites, they were attracted.

That had been four years ago now and whenever Beatrice's travels took them to London Rosie always sought out her sister. Her mother too had been quite happy to meet her long-estranged daughter, though Rosie suspected that her eagerness arose more from a desire to annoy her ex-husband than from any maternal longings. It hadn't been hard for Rosie to get to know her long-separated twin—she was so amazingly like their brilliant, charming and extremely selfish mother.

Morgan Urquart's eyes narrowed as he met the tigerish flow of his fiancée's eyes. 'I need a wife, not a soul mate.'

'Some people think the two are indivisible.'

'I'm not one of them.' The comment was sand-dry.

'I'm in total agreement.' Her sister's words echoed in her skull. 'Don't do anything to arouse his suspicion, Rosie, until Tuesday.' Now she'd met him she could appreciate the elaborate precautions that Elizabeth had felt it necessary to take. 'Shouldn't you go and see if Ellie is all right?'

'Are you trying to get rid of me, Elizabeth, after coming specially to see me?'

'She was very distressed.'

'All the more reason to keep out of her way,' he said cold-bloodedly, and began pacing up and down. 'The sooner this damned wedding is over and she and her mother are out from under my roof the better. You can hardly blame the child when the bloody woman fosters these fantasies. Amazingly convenient that my mother had no room under her own roof to house them,' he added with lazy cynicism.

'Did everyone expect you to marry her?' she asked curiously.

'My father and her father were best friends from prep school onwards. They did, I believe, conceive a half-baked theory that it would be tremendous if their offspring married.' The sound that emerged from his throat reflected his deepest scorn. 'The fact that they are now both dead and buried doesn't seem to have made any difference.'

'My condolences,' she murmured drily. He hardly sounded heartbroken. If he had a heart, this man kept it well hidden. He really was the most arrogant individual she'd ever encountered. The last grains of guilt she had felt at the subterfuge slipped away. Mr High and Mighty Urquart needed taking down a peg or two, and if she was there when it happened, fine! She found she could anticipate the event with pleasure.

He shot her a narrow, considering glance and stopped pacing the room. His immobility was more disturbing than his previous restlessness. 'Recent events, namely my grandfather's death, seem to have resurrected the idea.'

'It seems a bizarre thing to do—place such a stipulation in a will,' she said, momentarily distracted by her fascination to hear more about this peculiar family. 'To disinherit you if you don't marry within six months of his death.' Elizabeth had gleefully told her the bare facts behind this sudden desire for wedded bliss.

'Disinherit is a strong word. If I fail to abide by the terms of the will I will simply have to hand over my control of the company, or at least share it.'

'Shocking!' she murmured drily. When he looked at her sharply she simply opened her eyes wide, feigning innocence; irony was not a facet of Elizabeth's character that shone through.

'I could break it, of course,' he said, slumping with long-limbed elegance into a high-backed leather armchair. 'But the company would suffer in the interim; the family would rip it to pieces in their efforts to rescue it. On the whole it's simpler to marry you, and probably cheaper. By the way, I have the prenuptial agreement for you to show to your lawyer.' Her expression must have hinted at her repugnance at his attitude. 'The terms are generous.'

'I'm sure they are,' she said placidly. The cold-blooded arrogance of the man! Elizabeth had shown unusual wisdom in escaping this one. She longed to tell him exactly what she thought about his smug lack of humanity. Still, she'd have the opportunity very soon. Emotions were obviously too common for an Urquart, she thought, despising his aloof assumption of superiority. 'Wouldn't it have been just as easy to marry Ellie? Why me?'

'It's too late for second thoughts.' Despite his negligent posture she was sure he was suddenly extremely alert. He carried himself with an implacable authority that in itself was probably enough to quell any opposition.

'With such a generous future husband?' Her laugh was suitably vacuous. 'I'm just curious; she seemed to adore you. Isn't that what every man wants? A wife who worships him unconditionally?'

The faint air of someone wearily humouring a tiresome child was banished in a blink; a hardness slid into place and she glimpsed the steely predatory expression. If he'd been a rock-face there would have been no footholds, she decided, more awed by him than she dared admit to herself. 'A wife in love requires a great deal of attention, and besides, I like Ellie too much to marry her.'

She blinked, taking on board the casual insult with growing indignation. 'I infer from that that you don't like me, then?'

'Is that relevant? I know you, Elizabeth; you're the ideal wife for me,' he observed in a jaded way. He raised one long-fingered hand and ran his fingers through his pelt of gleaming hair, extending his neck as he did so as if to relieve tension in the strong muscles of his broad shoulders.

His grey eyes intercepted her stare and she shifted her gaze, uncomfortable at being caught gawping... He did have a singular, quite unique way of moving, breathtakingly co-ordinated, sleek, effortless grace in every mundane movement. She felt clumsy by comparison.

'It takes time to know someone.' Elizabeth had only been introduced to the man a month ago, she thought indignantly.

'I have a dossier on everything about you, my dear. I know all your secrets. Don't look so dismayed; it takes a lot to shock me and I wasn't looking for an *ingénue*.'

He obviously thought her horror stemmed from having her dark skeletons brought out for an airing, she realised incredulously.

'I want a woman who can be my hostess, mistress of my homes; you can do both. You know how to dress and behave and I believe you can be discreet about any... distractions you choose to indulge in. I'm positive you'll do nothing to embarrass me.' The silky warning in this final, seemingly pleasant remark was unmistakable.

'You've obviously given the matter considerable thought,' she said faintly. 'What if you fall in love?' She couldn't resist the question. With someone other than yourself, that is, she silently added, meeting his frowning regard blandly. 'It pays to be realistic when taking such a momentous step,' she explained solemnly.

'Realistically, the possibility of my falling in love—with anyone—is remote,' he said with breathtaking confidence. 'But as you seem to fall in and out of the over-worked term with such frequency I'm sure you'll compensate. And when I say anyone, Elizabeth, I include you,' he added, the rich voice coldly derisory. 'I have no wish for an entrée into your fantasy world.'

'The idea had never occurred to me,' she told him sincerely.

One darkly defined brow rose sardonically.

Rosie's anger and dislike were pushed past the bounds of common sense by the action...a strong case of the final straw, she was to decide later, when considering the day's events. She forgot all about being Elizabeth, who laughed off awkward situations and managed to get her own way by clever subterfuge, never confrontation.

'I have never been in love,' she announced, her teeth clenched and her jaw set at a pugnacious angle. 'If I ever do fall in love it will be with a man who is as different from you as is possible! So don't be concerned about the possibility of my putting you on a pedestal, because that is as unlikely as you falling in love!'

That was one pronouncement she didn't find any difficulty believing; tender emotions would be a foreign concept to this man. As her temper slid down to simmering level she recalled that she wasn't at that moment supposed to be speaking as herself but as her sister. She almost groaned out loud; if that self-indulgent outburst had ruined her twin's plan… 'I mean, I've never been properly in love,' she added, trying desperately to repair her slip.

'And after trying so often,' he observed drily, the contemplative frown caused by her outburst still knitting his brow.

Rosie flushed, wondering uncomfortably just how many things he knew about her twin that she didn't. What she *did* know was enough to raise the brows of the most liberal-minded. 'I'm surprised I was the lucky candidate, considering my track record.'

'It was because of your track record, Elizabeth,' he countered. 'I think the likelihood of your falling desperately in love and feeling inclined to terminate our contract before it suits me is slight. You like luxury and a certain lifestyle I can give you. Physically, I think I can keep you contented…it's not as though I'm demanding fidelity, just discretion.'

Unexpectedly he reached out and caught her hand. He examined the small palm and then turned it over and looked at her neat, unpolished nails. The sight seemed to fascinate him. Why should this casual if thorough contact affect her balance? she wondered as her head began to spin.

'When the child is old enough—' He broke off and looked at her enquiringly as she made a choked sound.

Utter disorientation paralysed her; her twin had conveniently left out several important details, she realised. This is only pretend, she kept telling herself; you won't be walking the aisle route in either direction with this man. Don't overreact, Rosie.

She gave a sudden laugh. At least he wasn't infallible, she realised, her sense of humour igniting—certainly not if he had chosen her sister from the available pedigrees he had no doubt waded through. Elizabeth a dutiful brood mare? She had the same lack of maternal instincts as their own mother, who had at frequent intervals explained what a barbaric process childbirth was…

And as for babies, Beatrice had said of them plaintively, 'They are so clinging!' She had strongly advised her daughters to avoid having children at all costs. So far she had been pleased with Rosie's lack of inclination to turn her into a grandmother—a situation that held no appeal.

'I seem to have amused you.'

Rosie tried to compose herself but one last husky chuckle escaped her. It was an attractive sound, low, warm and uninhibited. A sound Morgan Urquart had never heard before. An expression flickered in the depths of his cool grey eyes, but in a blink it had vanished.

'It's just difficult to imagine my…myself as a mother,' she said, deciding not to stray too far from the truth whenever possible. The occasional white lie she could pass off, but this sort of wholesale deception required character traits she was sadly lacking.

'The main reason for marriage is to provide myself with an heir.'

'I thought the main reason was to pander to your grandfather's dying wishes and keep control of the Urquart empire?' she said innocently.

He assimilated her audacious attack unblinkingly. His head went back and he regarded her from slightly narrowed eyes. Rosie silently likened the sensation to being a bug under a microscope and wished she'd kept her thoughts to herself. The hypocrisy of the man brought out the latent aggression in her normally placid personality; living with her mother as she did, there was little room for temperament; someone had to stay level-headed.

'The old man certainly liked to control people,' he said finally, wry admiration rather than resentment in his voice.

'I can understand it if you've rationalised your decision until it's something you wanted all along. It's so unpleasant to be manipulated, isn't it?' she observed with sweet sympathy. 'I think it's so wise of you to give in gracefully; it's much more dignified.'

His expression froze. 'You understand...?' he echoed. He sucked in his breath. 'I'm surprised that tongue of yours hasn't got you into serious trouble before now.'

'Marrying you might be considered that by certain enlightened folk.' She ought to have been regretting leaving her scripted role so far behind, but instead she felt a warm throb of elation as she smiled provokingly. If I'm really tiresome he might decide to call the whole thing off, she thought with sudden excitement. Why hadn't Elizabeth thought of that herself? It was so blissfully simple.

'From that comment am I to understand you are less than enamoured with the concept of becoming Mrs Urquart?'

'I would have preferred a title,' she said with a disgruntled expression. 'Still, you are a very old family,' she conceded reassuringly. He was watching her with a most peculiar expression—not precisely anger, she realised with disappointment. Elizabeth would be furious if she knew what her twin was doing, but Rosie felt quite marvellously self-indulgent at that moment.

'Extremely old,' he agreed gravely, and she noticed to her dismay that the initial impact of her manoeuvre had faded completely; he looked completely at ease. 'And tastelessly wealthy.'

'You'd have to be.' She discovered that the gleam of appreciative humour in his eyes was strangely attractive.

His laugh was dry-edged and grim. 'Don't push it... Elizabeth. I take it this is pique because I'm not inclined to smother you with compliments? Take comfort that whilst I am not moonstruck I find you an extremely attractive woman.'

His interpretation of her attitude as much as the intonation of his voice as he'd paid tribute to her—no, *Elizabeth's*—beauty made her feel hot and flustered. She let her head drop forward to shield the fact that she was blushing to the roots of her hair—like a schoolgirl, she thought with disgust.

'I may be pragmatic but I'm indulgent enough to make sure the task of procreation isn't too arduous.'

'For whom?' She raised her head, resentment quivering in her voice. He had to be the most conceited creature ever to draw breath. Was she…was Elizabeth supposed to be flattered by that comment?

'Challenge, Elizabeth…or invitation?' He got up and a sensation in the pit of her stomach uncoiled simultaneously, but with less control. He was a very tall man, muscular but not bulky, the strength of his body not flaunted but still evident.

She was intimidated, she acknowledged, trying to come to terms with the violent reaction that had immobilised her. Not by the physical threat of him, she realised, but by the expression that had heightened the scripted sensuality of his stern mouth and the explosive luminescence in the liquid grey eyes. She was filled with a sense of fascinated dread, and it was the unexpected thread of fascination that intimidated her still further…the warmth invading her limbs that terrified her.

'Neither,' she managed hoarsely as he loomed closer.

'Now that you've brought the subject up, I can't help but consider the inadvisability of marrying without first making quite certain that we are compatible in bed.' His voice had an insidious appeal despite the fact that his words filled her with horror. It was warm, vibrant and quite outrageously sensual.

'We only have a couple of days to wait.' This was a possibility she hadn't considered. How could she have been so short-sighted? she wondered, angered by her own stupidity. It hadn't even occurred to her to ask Elizabeth whether she had slept with the man...she evidently hadn't, and she, Rosie, wasn't going to either. Not even for her twin. Her constant underlying guilt that her sister had spent her childhood in a restrictive, unloving environment, whereas hers had been stimulating and exciting, tended to colour all her responses to her twin, but even guilt had its limits!

'Two days can seem such a long time.'

'Not long enough. I've a million things to do—dress fittings, caterers...' She stopped and clamped her lips together, aware that she was babbling. She could smell the distinctive male odour of his skin, warm, faint and disturbing. She took a deep breath and tried again. 'I came this morning because you invited me to an exhibition.'

'My mother's pet artist.' This distraction had at least delayed his intent, she saw with relief.

'Pet?' she said, her lips pursed with a disapproval that was echoed in her voice. 'What a very offensive term.' The look this comment earned her made her wish she could keep her unruly tongue under guard.

'You think so?' he said with a quirk of one dark brow. 'My mother collects artistic folk like some people collect stamps. It can prove to be a very expensive hobby,' he observed drily, with a sneer that set her hackles rising. 'Painters, sculptors, poets—all unappreciated and in need of an uncritical and wealthy patroness.'

'I take it your mother appreciates art more than you do,' she said primly.

'Con artists, the ones who latch on to my mother appear to be for the most part. Still, it keeps her happy,' he conceded carelessly. 'My father died when I was eight and I was never a suitable substitute for her manipulative attentions; she had to find appreciative substitutes.'

'My mother is an artist,' she reminded him stiffly, shocked by this casual indictment of his parent.

'Beatrice Lane. Do you have any contact with her?' he said, an expression of surprise on his face. 'I was under the impression—'

'The fact that I live with my father doesn't alter my pride in my mother's talent,' she said stiffly. Think Elizabeth, she told herself firmly, unable to prevent her own gut reaction to his implication that the artistic world was filled with poseurs and imposters.

'Your mother is a successful artist, almost an institution. My mother is only attracted to impoverished, unappreciated types.'

'Money gives respectability,' she drawled sarcastically.

'You've noticed that, too, have you?'

'Your mother sounds charming,' she added stubbornly, without the hard cynicism that characterised the woman's offspring.

'You didn't have a great deal to say to one another at dinner the other evening,' he observed drily, watching her with an expression that made Rosie dissolve into a morass of confused guilt.

'We hardly had a chance to get to know one another,' she replied shakily.

'Well, you can remedy that today, can't you?' To her surprise he didn't pursue the subject.

Rosie repressed a relieved sigh. Forty-eight hours suddenly seemed an awfully long time.

'I'll go and change,' he announced. 'I'll send in tea, shall I? Unless you prefer to help me, in a wifely way. I've never noticed you blush before; it's a formidable weapon in your arsenal.'

'Thank you, I'll cultivate it,' she said, willing her colour to fade. 'Tea will be sufficient,' she added politely.

He touched her jaw, a very light touch that made her pupils dilate and sent a violent shudder through her slender frame. Throat dry, stunned by the wild surge of emotion that swept through her body, she watched the laughing expression that had momentarily lit his eyes fade. 'As you wish,' he said stiffly, and removed himself from the room.

Rosie sank into a sofa and tried to cope with the trembling reaction to her first encounter with Morgan Urquart. Having teeth pulled suddenly seemed light relief by comparison. When bare minutes later the youthful and freshly scrubbed Ellie appeared she almost groaned.

'I suppose you think you're so clever,' the girl sneered, getting straight to the point.

Rosie, who had just been contemplating the abysmal lack of intelligence she had been showing, smiled placatingly. The girl really did look a great deal better without the make-up, she decided, looking directly and calmly into the stormy young face.

'You'll win no Brownie points with Morgan by performing further melodramas,' she said, not unkindly.

This advice went down particularly badly; twin patches of colour appeared on each of the girl's cheeks. 'I suppose you had a good laugh about me!' she accused. 'He doesn't love you and never will.'

Rose felt helpless. She could hardly obey her first impulse and inform the girl that she could think of worse fates at that particular moment. She remained silent.

'He still loves Rachel, his first wife.' The malicious smile that curved the wilful mouth became victorious as Rosie betrayed surprise. 'He'll never love anyone else, everyone knows that, but I could make him happy. You're just a little trollop.'

Rosie wondered who she was quoting on that point but wisely didn't enquire. 'Possibly, but the ring is on my finger,' she said gently, pointing to the enormous diamond that nestled on her left hand.

The girl looked about to burst into tears once more. 'His secretary probably bought it.' She departed as swiftly as she had entered, almost ploughing down the maid who was bringing Rosie tea.

Rosie sipped the delicate brew after the girl withdrew and tried to regain her equilibrium. Some of the information Ellie had thrown at her was surprising. So Morgan had been married before and wasn't now?

In the grip of a strong curiosity, she wished she could call Ellie back and dig further details from her. Not, she reminded herself, that Morgan Urquart was any concern of hers; two short days and she'd be out of his life for good. Considering the lacerated state of her nervous system after an hour, she dreaded to think what state she'd be in by then.

With this daunting thought she replaced the delicate china cup on the tray and attacked the plate of biscuits.

CHAPTER TWO

WHEN ROSIE SAW THE GALLERY Morgan was taking her to she considered bitterly how unkind fate was being to her today. Her mother had held her last, highly successful London exhibition here, and Rosie, in her role as combined secretary, agent and general girl Friday, had made all the arrangements with the gallery owner. She was sure to be recognised. Beatrice Lane relied on her daughter to organise every detail of her nomadic lifestyle.

Still, I am Elizabeth, she recalled, subduing the sense of panic that made her reluctant to get out of the deep leather-upholstered seat of the car. If people expect Elizabeth, that's what they see, she thought, obeying Morgan's rather impatient gesture to use the door he held open for her. She slithered out, the snug-fitting skirt Elizabeth had chosen for her riding up to reveal the lace-topped stocking she wore. She tugged at the fabric and glanced around, hoping her inelegance was not being noted.

Morgan's eyes were fixed intently on the exposed curve of her thigh, his expression hidden from her view but his interest obvious. Angrily, she adjusted the garment modestly and completed her transfer. When Morgan raised his eyes she glimpsed a disturbing, restless, hungry look which immediately became wryly humorous as he encountered her angry glare.

Hand in the small of her back, he guided her through the open external glass doors of the gallery. 'Do you do that unconsciously, or just when you want to whet an appetite?'

he said softly, inclining his head towards her and nodding casually to an aquaintance.

'Do what?' she enquired suspiciously, her eyes scanning the fashionably dressed gathering for faces she recognised, and, more importantly, that would recognise her. She felt strangely self-conscious walking into a room at Morgan's side; eyes turned to look at him with the same predictability as the moon's rising—a fact which probably accounted for the cynical twist to his lips which was almost, but not quite, a sneer. Being thrust unwillingly into the limelight made her uncomfortable and emphasised in her guilty mind the deceit she was perpetrating.

'Give a tantalising glimpse of what the cookie jar has to offer. Lace, leg and miles of flesh,' he added, just in case she hadn't got his drift. His breath actually stirred the fine hair on the nape of her neck as he leaned closer, his attitude one of casual intimacy.

She took a deep, wrathful breath and refused to let herself dissolve into incoherent embarrassment. 'It was purely accidental, nothing personal,' she said, adopting a faintly puzzled attitude. Was he deliberately trying to needle her?

The dark brows became a straight line of disapproval. 'As my wife, it's the sort of accident you had best neglect.'

'I thought it was quite subtle,' she protested mildly.

'Are you trying to—?' He caught her chin and forced her to meet his dispassionate stare.

'Morgan! So you managed to get here, and only an hour late. How delightful.' The crisp, ironic voice at Rosie's shoulder interrupted whatever Morgan was about to say.

'I was up all night, Mother,' he said, the explanation in no way an apology. His hand fell from Rosie's face but he retained a grip on her arm. Considering his lack of subterfuge about the circumstances that had led him to marriage, the public display of ownership was something of an unpleasant shock to Rosie.

The woman's eyes, a deeper grey than her son's, grew

colder as they touched Rosie. 'Spare me the details,' she drawled with some of the hauteur she'd passed on to her son.

Taking immediate exception to the derision in this brief scrutiny, Rosie felt herself instinctively stiffen. If Morgan's earlier comments had led her to expect someone warm and sympathetic, a sort of fluffy, gullible, motherly type, then this tall, slender person with the perfect grooming and austere cast to her features dispelled this illusion. Rosie couldn't imagine this woman being duped by anyone.

'Business, not pleasure kept me up, Mother, and as always I will spare you the details.'

'Your life lacks balance.'

'Let me be the judge of that, Mother.' His patience was obviously wearing thin. He and his mother carried the identical air of people who didn't suffer fools at all, and certainly not gladly.

'I want to talk to you...alone.'

Manners were not high on the Urquart agenda, Rosie thought wrathfully. 'Don't mind me; I'll mingle,' she said, her calm tone at variance with the sparkle of anger that lit her eyes. I'm Elizabeth...I'm Elizabeth. She kept up the litany in her head, ignoring the wave of a dealer she recognised. I don't have to believe it so long as Morgan does, she reminded herself.

'Do look at the pictures, dear.' The patronising malice in the older woman's voice made her fingers curl into small, tight fists.

'I almost forgot,' she said vaguely. 'The pictures...' Her sister played the empty-headed bimbo with abandon when it suited her, and at that moment Rosie could appreciate why. She realised how fortunate she was in never having been judged solely on her appearance.

This response elicited the expected degree of scorn from the older woman, but the shrewd look Morgan directed at her was almost amused. She acknowledged fretfully that he was too sharp to fool easily—and he managed to zero in on her dry humour, which was something many people missed.

'Promising, don't you think, Rosie?'

She nodded automatically as a familiar voice spoke in her ear. 'Extremely...' she began, then she gave a small shriek. 'Gunther, what are you...?' The bear hug was vigorous enough to inhibit her breathing. People, she realised, pulling away, were staring in an amused, benevolent sort of way at the slender, dark-haired girl being crushed by the large bear of a man.

'I might ask you the same question, Rosie, or should I say Elizabeth?'

'You're not going to give me away, are you?'

'Are you fluttering your lashes like that to get around me or keep in character?' he enquired, and Rosie gave a gurgle of reluctant laughter.

'Both,' she admitted, and it was her companion's turn to laugh. An awful thought occurred to her. 'Is Mother here?' she said, willing herself not to look over her shoulder furtively. That really would put the cat amongst the pigeons.

'Your mother is aboard a yacht in the Aegean.'

'And why aren't you with her?' she asked swiftly, sensing undercurrents.

'I don't care to compete with young Adonises, and the sun burns me. Besides, I happen to be the new owner of this gallery.'

'You!' she ejaculated. 'That's quite a diversification from electronics.' Gunther, her mother's most dedicated suitor, was extremely rich, but Rosie's grasp of his interests was vague. However, she knew that art had not been one of them—up to this point.

'I could do with a manager. The present incumbent has been head-hunted,' he said, acknowledging her observation with a slight smile. 'Care for the job?'

'I have a job.' She gave him a puzzled frown. Despite

the procession of young men, embarrassingly young at times, that slipped in and out of her mother's life, Gunther was a permanent fixture, his role ambiguous but essential. His expression at the moment confused her.

'Pity,' he said casually. 'If you weren't around, my dear, I think it's possible Beatrice might appreciate me a little more. You make her too comfortable.' She couldn't tell if the accusation was entirely serious, but it troubled her. 'Anyway, what have you been up to? Aren't you a little old for charades? I asked about the charming young lady and was told she was Miss *Elizabeth* Osborne, who was soon to be a member of the Urquart dynasty.'

'How did you know it was me?'

'An inclination of the head...a way of moving. Perhaps I know the girl underneath the new clothes rather too well to be so easily deceived.'

'You have been keeping yourself amused, I see.'

'Morgan, this is...' Her entire body had tensed as she'd heard the silky observation. Spinning around, her expression almost comically guilty, she met the predatory expression on her escort's face and her voice lost its impetus entirely and faded away. She had the distinct impression that he'd heard Gunther's last comment and she could well imagine what interpretation he had placed on it. A portion of her mind registered anger at his presumption of ownership whilst she fought a burgeoning guilty blush.

'Gunther, I didn't know you were in the country.' She watched with growing dismay as the two men shook hands. Despite the fact that the German was a head shorter than Morgan, he was vastly broad across the shoulders, a powerful dynamo of a man with harsh but expressive features and a shock of dark hair streaked with grey. Even as the eldest of her mother's suitors he was still a couple of years Beatrice's junior, being a little over forty.

'I bought the gallery actually, Morgan, so you can relax.

I'm not here to steal a march on any of your deals. I am here simply to display proprietorial interest.'

'I make sure my interests are protected against pirates.' Morgan's eyes touched Rosie and she realised with despairing annoyance that this conversation was taking place on two levels. Macho men—give me strength! she thought. 'I take it you've met Elizabeth?'

Gunther's eyes met hers for a split second and she held her breath. 'Not formally,' he said, and with a gallantry that made her want to giggle he bent over solemnly, his lips briefly saluting her shapely hand. A frown formed as he took in the ostentatious diamond that sat loosely on her finger. 'I know Elizabeth's sister very well; the resemblance is bewildering,' he added, impervious to the silent signals she was flashing him.

'We're only engaged for a couple more days,' Morgan supplied as the older man straightened up. He had been watching the interplay, his face inscrutable. His hand came up suddenly to snake around Rosie's waist, drawing her closer to him. He stood with feet apart, apparently at ease, but the ruthless strength in the arm effectively chaining her to his side was anything but casual. 'If you're still in the country I can arrange an invite.'

'Kind of you...both, but I have previous commitments,' Gunther said, his accent slightly more pronounced than usual. Rosie avoided meeting his gaze, unable to cope with the questions and concern she would see there.

'I'd like to sample some of that buffet,' she said, speaking to Morgan. 'Lovely to meet you, Mr...?'

'Weiss, Gunther Weiss. I hope you both enjoy yourselves.' He watched them move away with a frown of deep concern. He saw Rosie detach herself from the tall, distinctive figure and gracefully fly back to him through the crush.

'I'll explain later, tonight at your apartment,' she whispered furtively, picking up her clutch bag from the table beside them. 'Here it is,' she said in a louder voice, and held it aloft, waving to Morgan, who was watching them, his dark blond hair easily discernible above the mêlée. His eyes were narrowed in hard contemplation and she looked away.

Rosie was breathless and flushed by the time she reattached herself to his side. 'I found it,' she said, hiding her nervousness behind a brilliant smile.

'You appear to find Gunther very…stimulating. I've rarely seen you so animated,' he remarked impassively. 'I've heard you described as reckless,' he commented, picking up a glass of champagne from the table they'd reached.

'Is that so?' she said brightly, draining her glass in one gulp; sedation seemed sensible under the circumstances.

'When you're my wife I'd recommend curbing your enthusiasm for danger,' he said casually, replacing his glass without tasting the sparkling liquid.

'The job description gets more tedious every time I hear a new clause,' she snapped back. Her guilt at deceiving him had receded considerably. Getting the upper hand with this awful man was a pleasant prospect.

The grey eyes were at their most expressionless, glittering and totally remorseless. 'If you'd realised that sooner we'd both be happier. However, a certain sequence of events has been set in motion.' There was a definite warning in his words.

'Do events always turn out the way you want?' The scorn she injected into her voice made him compress his lips. Suddenly she knew she wasn't going to pass herself off as Elizabeth when she gave him his marching orders. She wanted him to know just what a fool he'd been; the omnipotent Morgan Urquart had been taken for a ride by a mere female and she—Rosie—was that female.

No one in her life had ever made her this angry. She could hear the blood throbbing in her ears. Serve him right if she actually jilted him at the altar! The outrageously awful idea sobered her; the thought that she could dislike anyone that badly made her feel physically nauseous.

'Eventually, always,' he confirmed. 'You really are a child, aren't you...Elizabeth? Pushing...to see how far you can safely go. I take it this little display is for my benefit? You're hardly being subtle.'

Was that an odd inflection in his voice as he said her name? Her imagination was working overtime; she firmly shook off this idea. If he knew, he'd hardly be going along with her, would he? 'I'm merely enjoying myself,' she said airily. 'I've not the faintest idea what you're talking about.'

'I never doubted you're enjoying yourself. However, I'm not enjoying the spectacle.'

And that would never do, would it? she thought, his words igniting the smouldering anger that his casual cavalier attitude had kept banked up. 'Tough,' she muttered truculently.

'Would you care to repeat that comment?'

His anger filled her with a passionate satisfaction. 'Certainly...' Her voice faded and her eyes grew round with horror as she realised what she'd been doing. Keeping her head low, arousing no suspicions—that had been her remit. What had possessed her to bait him like this? 'I may not be the lovesick bride, but it can be humiliating to be summarily dismissed like a child. I expect to be treated with some respect. Your mother obviously loathes me,' she said, choosing her words with care.

The fact that she had feelings would be news to him, she thought, trying to control the righteous indignation that made her want to snap him out of his smug complacence.

If any man deserved to be left standing at the altar he did, she thought wistfully. Am I really considering...? Her eyes opened wide with shock as she realised that was exactly what she had been contemplating.

'My mother will accept you in time,' Morgan said with a hint of impatience. 'I would never have imagined you were that fragile. Do other people's opinions matter so much?'

A passing group of people pushed into her, sending her straight at him. His arms opened and she was held steady against his chest.

The impact alone couldn't account for the breathless sensation. Her concentration was ripped into shreds and cast to the winds. There was an unexpected tension in him and she couldn't help but be affected—at least that was what she later told herself. A static electricity that crackled between them made him stiffen. A sound halfway between a purr and growl vibrated in his chest and she felt a ripple pass through his body, a wave of muscular contraction. At this point she pulled away, every nerve-ending in her body screaming in protest as she put space between them.

She wasn't even aware of the slight negative gesture she made before pinning a strained smile to her lips. It had taken just seconds to shatter her composure but it took a little longer to retrive it. 'So crowded in here.' That was as far as she intended going in reference to the incident. 'It would be easier if your family liked me.'

'They're a pack of hyenas.'

This casual announcement succeeded in drawing Rosie's deliberately restless gaze back to his face. 'How comforting…' she began. The expression on his face was intense, analytical, that of a man who had discovered a discrepancy in his accounts and was looking for the error. Those eyes were as ruthless as a surgeon's scalpel.

'We're not a close family,' he observed, shifting his gaze, much to her relief, to a painting they were now standing beside. 'But then your own family is divided.'

Rosie concentrated on the raw explosion of colour on the canvas, sensing his eyes on her face. 'My sister and I keep in touch.'

'But you had no contact as children?'

'None,' she admitted sadly. The loss of those years always left a bitter taste in her mouth.

'Difficult for twins. Identical, aren't you?' he said casually. 'No psychic links?'

She ignored the sarcasm. 'I'm the elder by four minutes.' Am I imagining the undertones? she wondered, willing her voice to stay casual. He sounded almost sympathetic.

'I thought you told me your sister—what's her name... Ruth?—was the eldest.'

'Rosie. You must have been mistaken.' She rubbed the bridge of her nose and eyed him calmly. He smiled back languidly, as if he wasn't giving her his entire concentration, and she breathed again.

'Are they able to attend the wedding?'

'Mother is a bit of a gypsy. She's hard to track down sometimes but I'll keep trying. She's hopping round the Greek islands at the moment.'

'And does your sister always tag along?'

Awake to every nuance, she was sure she detected a sneer. 'She's devoted,' Rosie agreed drily, without a pause. She wouldn't mind strangling Morgan Urquart with his own superiority, she decided. Humbling him was a proposition that was oh, so tempting.

'The famous usually have a retinue of hangers-on.'

This observation made her stumble. 'Ridiculous heels,' she snapped, shrugging off his hand. 'My sister acts as secretary,' she said. The smile was in danger of becoming permanently fixed and her cheek muscles ached abominably. Secretary...! She had total control of the financial side of her mother's life, and she made sure that everything else ran like clockwork. As Beatrice often said fondly, Rosie had become indispensable.

'No offence intended; you seem very protective of your sister. Couldn't you leave a message at their home address? Surely someone there would be able to contact them.'

'Home! My mother has a place in Lucerne but she is

there one month out of every twelve. She visits friends, travels, never stays in one place long.'

'She is prolific,' he remarked, listening to this description with only minimal interest. 'I wouldn't have thought that sort of lifestyle would be conducive to work.'

'She needs constant stimulation; it's a formula that works and she sees no reason to alter it—at least that's what Rosie tells me,' she added. 'I don't know my mother that well.'

'You must envy your sister for having seen the world.'

A spasm of something akin to pain crossed her features and she lowered her chin in automatic defence. And, composure or not, there was still a suspicious glimmer in her amber eyes and a defiant edge to her voice as she replied. 'Several times, I shouldn't wonder.'

A home, somewhere that was her own at the end of the day... She'd outgrown her childish resentment at being shipped about with as little thought or consideration as her mother's paints—probably less, she thought, considering her odd upbringing with a small, wry smile.

School had been the one touch of stability, but when Beatrice had become aware of her daughter's organisational skills she had announced that she couldn't possibly do without her any longer. 'Seventeen is much too old for a stuffy girls' school,' she had explained, promising Rosie a lifestyle that would be the envy of all her friends.

Morgan watched her face and the restless flicker of emotion that ran over it with a grim if complacent expression. 'Do you want to leave now? I think you've done your duty.'

She looked up jerkily; something in the melodic purr of his velvety voice evoked a spurt of irrational fear within her. The flicker of anger she thought she saw in his eyes was probably a trick of the light, she decided, because he looked bland, almost benevolent, as he returned her stare. 'If you wouldn't mind,' she said with relief.

He put her in a taxi and made no effort to join her in

the back. 'I'll see you later on.' He raised a quizzical brow at her blank expression tinged with panic. 'Surely you haven't forgotten our dinner engagement?'

'Of course not,' she improvised swiftly.

'I'll pick you up at eight.'

'No, I'll meet you...there.' She had other things to do this evening—and where was 'there'?

'As you wish—the usual place.'

'Usual?'

With a half-reproachful look he named a French restaurant she had heard of. 'Of course,' she stumbled, nodding to the driver to move on...quickly. She didn't see the shade of cynical amusement that lit Morgan's eyes as he waved her off.

ELIZABETH'S BEDROOM was opulent, expensive and chaotically untidy. Rosie doubted her sister even noticed it. She sat on the canopied bed feeling like an intruder in the room. With a sigh she leaned her head on her knees. The morning had been a nightmare but no one except Gunther had caught on to her deception.

Elizabeth had predicted that their father would accept her without question, and she'd been right; it had required no special subterfuge on her part. The more contact she had with him, the more she marvelled at the optimism which had made her parents believe their union could survive. Love was not only blind, she decided, getting up, but stupid!

She'd survived the first part of the day—the awful exhibition followed by a fitting for her wedding dress. Though inclined to miss that, she had known it would arouse suspicion were she to do so. The fact that the dress was too snug across her bust had caused a minor furore and the designer had been livid with her underlings—something which Rosie had felt extremely guilty about.

Standing for hours with pins poking into awkward spots,

she'd imagined Morgan's face if she actually let him get as far as the altar. The sniggers and malicious sympathy would be impossible for someone as stiff-necked and proud as he was to take.

He deserves it; why waste any sympathy on that overbearing tyrant? she thought. He deserves everything he gets, she decided, very tempted to do what the devil in her head suggested.

Choosing a sapphire silk sheath from her sister's vast selection of clothes, she wondered at this vindictive streak she seemed to have developed overnight. One minute she had convinced herself she'd simply be Elizabeth and get out a respectable time before the wedding, and the next...

Slipping the dress over her head, she regarded her reflection in one of the mirrors which made it impossible not to see herself from every corner of the room. It was simple, just a shift, but it emphasised the youthful, curvaceous promise of her body and made her legs and arms appear even more graceful and slender.

'What am I contemplating?' she wondered out loud. The rancour and resentment she felt was not just on her sister's behalf. She was honest enough to acknowledge that that man goaded her more than anyone in her experience.

She turned her head and her hair swished like a curtain around her face before settling into the straight, silken cascade that ended on her shoulderblades. As Rosie, it would be tied back in a neat braid or an elegant chignon; but tonight she was Elizabeth, a fact which made her add another dab of colour to her cheeks and be more flamboyant with the colour she outlined her generous lips with.

A dinner date with her supposed fiancé had come as a nasty shock; that was one engagement her twin had omitted to mention, she thought resentfully. She wished her stomach weren't quivering with nervous tension as she summoned a cab and gave him directions to Gunther's flat. She and her mother had stayed in the Georgian terrace on several occasions.

Gunther himself opened the door. He was towelling his hair and he beckoned her into the first-floor drawing room to wait for him.

It was an hour later before she'd finished explaining the story to him, and his expression was not promising.

'I've never known you to be so rash before,' he observed in his rather guttural voice. 'I don't think you quite realise what sort of man you're dealing with. Morgan can be ruthless in achieving his own ends. When he took over the family firm it was about to go under—general apathy and too many chiefs. He was already established in the States as a major influence in the computer industry; the man is a software genius. Combine that with his business acumen…!'

He shrugged his massive shoulders expressively. 'I'm not surprised he doesn't want to hand over control; he *is* the company; without Morgan the rest of his family would run it back into the ground. One of the provisos when he invested his own capital to save the firm was that he had complete control, and the old man agreed. With his death the obligation has been set aside. At least that is the story on the grapevine, and Elizabeth's tale would seem to confirm this.'

'I had to help Elizabeth,' she insisted stubbornly, secretly dismayed by his response and the information he'd given her. Was helping Elizabeth the only reason she was stubbornly resisting calling a halt to this charade? Hadn't it all become more personal to her? She was offended by everything about Morgan and she wanted to thwart him in a way he'd never forget.

'You have an over-developed sense of obligation, Rosie; I have always thought so. Be selfish,' he advised. 'It could be the same sort of obligation that brought Morgan back to this country and made him turn Urquart Enterprises into a software company to rival any. He had already been treated unfairly on the previous occasion when he returned to the fold. They expected him to work his way quietly up the ranks.'

'Seems reasonable,' she said obstinately.

'Morgan is not a man happy to sit by and let less talented people decide his fate; the frustration must have been intolerable. Tell him tonight; don't prolong this farce,' he advised sternly.

'Elizabeth asked me to wait until tomorrow; she'll feel safer. Besides,' she added, her eyes glowing. 'I'd love to see that manipulative rat have a taste of his own medicine! He doesn't give a damn about Elizabeth. He was going to ruin her life!' Her voice trembled with emotion—too much emotion, a troubled voice in her head observed; but she was not in a mood to listen to either that or Gunther's sober warnings.

'I hope for your sake that's just a desire, not an intention,' Gunther said flatly. 'You are forgetting that Elizabeth entered into this arrangement of her own volition. Unless I misunderstood you, Rosie, she knew this was no love match…she must take at least half the blame, maybe more. Was she not using him?'

'People like Morgan Urquart rarely get what they deserve,' she observed with a small, stiff smile. She got up, brushing down her dress with an unsteady hand. 'It would be nice if just for once he did. Are you going to give me away?' she asked tremulously. She didn't see any advantage in antagonising Gunther; she needed his co-operation, or at least his temporary silence.

'I should.' The tone was rueful.

'You're an angel,' she said, flashing him a smile of relief. 'Don't worry,' she told him, emerging from a hug minutes later as they stood at the open door. 'I know exactly what I'm doing to the nice Mr Urquart.'

'If Morgan was nice I would not be concerned,' Gunther told her darkly.

As Rosie walked along the pavement to her waiting taxi she tried to throw off the sensation in the pit of her stomach that told her she ought to have listened to Gunther and not her own instincts.

'What a pleasant surprise, darling.' Morgan made the endearment sound particularly unpleasant. He paid off the waiting cab driver, who, despite her instinctive cry of alarm, left her to her fate—after one comprehensive glance at her companion, that was.

Morgan didn't look like a man to push too far, she had to concede. Tall and wolf-lean, clad in a leather jacket and snug-fitting jeans, he presented a very dangerous package of refined power, which was complicated, for her at least, by the very unrefined sexuality that emanated from him. It was raw, and curiously offensive to her. She still hadn't recovered the power of speech as the cab disappeared from view.

'What are you doing here? Don't frogmarch me,' she added belligerently as she was hustled along the pavement. His response to this, after a considering glance from unfriendly cold grey eyes, was to take the matter of locomotion quite literally out of her hands—or rather off her feet.

It would, she knew, be extremely undignified to struggle, although the impulse to escape was almost overwhelming. He loped along as though his arms were not full of her. She tried to hold herself rigid; she was certainly furious, alarmed, but despite all that the temptation to let her cheek rest on his shoulder was alarmingly strong.

He dumped her unceremoniously in the seat of a low-slung coupé parked across the street and slammed the door, permitting himself a tell-tale excess of force in the action.

'How dare you?' she breathed as he slid in beside her. 'I am not one of those women who find it enthralling to be treated like a bag of potatoes. Save the sort of activity for females who would no doubt swoon in the face of all that masculine strength,' she snarled sarcastically. 'I've always wondered how women can be attacked in the middle of a busy area whilst all and sundry look on. Now I know.'

'Fasten your seat belt and shut up,' he advised, without even affording her the courtesy of looking at her.

'I will not—' she began furiously.

'You're so predictable it becomes tedious,' he observed as he leant across her and clicked the seat belt in place.

The movement brought his torso into close contact with her lightly clad body. She knew then exactly how a cat felt if its fur had been stroked the wrong way; even the invisible downy hairs on her skin felt painful with a weird and unpleasant combination of aversion and hypersensitivity. She was unaware of her suspended breath until he straightened up; but, from the brief but comprehensive glance he gave her whilst he was doing so, she realised he wasn't. In fact, she fancifully imagined that nothing at all escaped those alarming eyes.

What interpretation had he put on her overreaction? she wondered, not choosing to analyse it herself at that moment. 'I'm sorry if I bore you,' she said, her voice as stiff as her posture. 'Only I feel some explanation for your bizarre behaviour is necessary.'

'I might say the same,' he said, and the look he flashed her made her belatedly aware that her farewell to Gunther had been witnessed and duly misinterpreted. There would be a certain irony in explaining her behaviour to a man who didn't even know her name, she mused.

'How did you just happen to be outside?' Attack was infinitely preferable to defence, she decided.

If she'd been hoping to faze him she was doomed to disappointment. 'I followed you,' he supplied matter-of-factly. 'You were in there an hour and fifteen minutes and it looked as though you were reluctant to leave,' he observed, cataloguing her movements without expression.

'That's sick,' she accused. 'You're no better than a peeping Tom.'

'I'm a fiancé who takes exception to my bride-to-be flaunting her lover in public. Did you really expect me to believe you'd never seen Gunther before this morning?' he asked, his tone derisory. 'It was obvious this morning you were close…*very* close.'

'Why should you care if I have a thousand lovers? Our marriage is to be one of convenience; but quite how convenient it will be for me is becoming increasingly vague. Discretion was the key word, as I recall,' she drawled. The hypocrisy of the man was breathtaking. 'Didn't your definitive study of my life include details of Gunther?' she enquired scornfully.

It seemed to Rosie that she was paying for her sister's foolishness, and she was becoming increasingly resentful of the fact. It was about time Morgan started suffering, she decided, with more emotion than logic. He was now firmly entrenched in her mind as the guilty party.

'We'll discuss it when we get there.'

'Would it be too much to ask where "there" is?' she enquired with pointed sarcasm. 'Not to the restaurant, I take it?'

'I have a house in Suffolk. I hadn't planned to use it so we'll have to fend for ourselves.'

'"We"!' she shrieked. 'Where did you get this "we"? You can go wherever you like, but I have not the slightest intention of going with you.'

'I don't recall giving you an option,' he said in a tone reserved for humouring imbeciles.

She stared in angry frustration at his profile. 'I realise the Urquarts feel they're closely related to God, but this, by any standards, is atrocious behaviour. Stop this car right now,' she demanded, her voice throbbing with emotion.

'I'll bring you back to town in the morning. Right now we need to sort out a few ground rules with no interruptions.' His eyes shone like some cold, polished metal as he flicked her a sideways glance of irritation, and she shuddered.

'That sounds sinister,' she replied, refusing to be intimidated or to acknowledge that she felt a flurry of undiluted panic. 'Am I supposed to be cowed?' she enquired, her throat dry and her heart pounding.

'You, Rosie, are supposed to be quiet.' Soft, deadly, the casual words hit her like a blow in the solar plexus.

'What did you call me?' High-pitched and breathless, her question was little more than a whisper.

'Rosie Osborne.'

She listened to his dry voice, the world quietly falling to pieces around her. Questions stumbled over one another in her spinning head. One emerged. 'How?' She had already recognised that denial was futile.

The laugh hinted at a cruelty she had already seen in that single dismissive glance. 'For starters, how about this...?' He took one hand off the steering wheel and caught hold of one of her hands, which were tensely clenched in her lap. 'Your sister would have died before she'd have gone out in public with nails like this. I knew the very first time I saw them.'

He let her go and Rosie gazed at her trembling fingers—short nails, innocent of polish—and realised how true that statement was. All the time she'd imagined she'd been fooling him, even contemplated allowing her resentment to take the charade further than ever intended, he'd known! Humiliation washed over her like a tidal wave.

'Detail is so important, but even without obvious slips like that your performance was not about to win any Oscars. Incidentally, Elizabeth and I do not have a "usual place" and we did not have any arrangement concerning this evening. Homework is vital if you want to play a role properly.'

'Just stop the car,' she said, feeling sick. 'You're far too clever, I admit that. Are you satisfied?'

'You think you can walk away?' He gave a short laugh of disbelief. 'Consequences, Rosie; you really should have considered the consequences,' he chided mockingly.

'I don't know what you mean!' Trapped, cornered—she felt both, and her mind refused to work.

He smiled in a way she was beginning to loathe, and she expelled a pent-up shaky breath. 'All in good time.'

He wasn't about to be drawn; she could see that. He'd tell her what was on his mind only after he'd made her suffer as much as possible. Let him have his moment. She had to admit that, from his point of view, she'd probably earned some sort of chastisement. There had been clues, she told herself angrily; there must have been. Only she'd been too busy indulging her own private concept of an eye for an eye. She'd been too smug and complacent to perceive disaster on the horizon.

She'd just have to bide her time and keep her cool. She'd fallen to pieces on cue, just as he'd intended, but he was about to learn that Rosie Osborne wasn't one of his minions. What was the worst he could do to her…?

CHAPTER THREE

MORGAN'S RURAL RETREAT lay at the end of an unsurfaced track along which she had been jolted for what seemed like miles. The outline of the building indicated a moderate-sized, partly thatched house.

The interior revealed olde-world charm by the bucketful, but Rosie was in no mood to appreciate it. Though it did occur to her as she glanced around that it wasn't the sort of place she would have imagined appealed to him. Too chintzy by far.

'An aunt left it to me,' he said, as if reading her thoughts, as she followed him further inside. 'I've never got around to selling it and it does have the useful advantage of making me inaccessible.'

'You do surprise me. I took you for the sentimental type.' Her calm disdain might have surprised him; she couldn't tell; that film of ice in his eyes was impossible to see beyond. The mention of inaccessibility had alerted her to the full vulnerability of her situation, but she fought a successful battle to keep her apprehension concealed behind a calm expression. 'Keeping me here won't alter the fact that Elizabeth has dumped you. In fact, right now she's probably…'

'Mrs William Maguire,' he smilingly supplied, one dark brow quirked at her open-mouthed expression.

'How did you…?' The fact that he must have been aware of her deception almost from the outset was horrifying; now he was making it clear that he knew the reasons behind that deception. As if responding to some primitive radar her eyes were drawn to his grey regard; the dispassionate cruelty she saw there was far worse than any hot rage. His motivation in whisking her off like this had never seemed likely to be benevolent, but, now that he'd revealed that he knew her identity and more, she was seriously alarmed.

'It didn't strain my resources to trace what your sister had been getting up to. I already knew about Bill Maguire, though I readily admit I imagined he was history.' The wall lights he'd switched on in the hallway cast shadows which emphasised the sculpted contours of his austere features, lending them a distinctly sinister appearance in her sensitive eyes.

'She loves him.'

'He has my sincere sympathy,' he said with mock formality, inclining his head. 'Duplicity and deception are not attributes generally inclined to make a good wife,' he observed harshly.

'There speaks the expert,' she said, throwing her hair back with a sharp jerk of her jaw—a jaw which ached with tension. She eyed him hostilely. She'd hit a nerve; it was evident in the tautening of his already rigid facial muscles, the flicker of light in his eyes and the nerve that pulsed erratically in his lean cheek. She assimilated the finely tuned alterations—minute, but telling. At the same instant she recalled the jealous teenager's taunts about his first wife.

'A man who rides roughshod over everyone is not exactly one I'd choose to cherish me, and it's fairly obvious Elizabeth grasped that fact too, if belatedly. I'd wager that the first Mrs Urquart led a less than blissful existence.'

'Naturally I find your opinions profoundly interesting,' he said in a bored tone; but she could see that the bland manner was purely superficial—his eyes had narrowed to slits as she'd made her last comment. 'Your attitude is unfortunate. Still, I feel sure you'll make the best of it, under the circumstances.' He only paused long enough to see her freeze, before turning and casually walking away.

She caught up with him in the kitchen, which lay at the end of the long, narrow passageway. It was a small fitted galley, given the illusion of space by a conservatory dining area which opened directly from it, and which no doubt opened up onto a garden. But it was just a black void at that moment—much like the one in the pit of her stomach.

'Don't walk off like that,' she said. Her voice sounded strangely breathless in her ears. Her heart was working at a rate that made her head feel light. Adrenalin-charged, she faced him, a slender wand of outrage, as apprehension and plain fear were transformed into fury of a reckless variety.

'It's an excellent sign—this craving for my company.'

Her teeth gouged a groove in her lower lip. 'I'd sooner seek the company of a starving wolf.' He flashed her a derisory look and continued to pour coffee beans into a grinder; the pungent odour filled her flared nostrils. 'Much rather,' she added, her voice saturated with sincerity. Her eyes, filled with loathing, were fixed on the dull gold sheen of his bent head. Was he sadistic or just completely indifferent to anyone else's feelings? she wondered.

'I'm curious as to how far you intended to go with this substitution,' he said, abandoning his task and turning the full force of his gaze upon her. 'To the altar, or beyond...? To what extent did you intend to immerse yourself in the role?' he mused, watching her flinch with cold amusement. 'Had you intended to slip that tantalising body between my sheets?'

As he spoke the inherent musicality of his voice was deeply apparent; even her fingertips responded tinglingly to the sound, she realised with blank amazement. The meaning of his almost casual and definitely derogatory words offended her, as did the slow journey his eyes made over her body. Her dress seemed suddenly flagrantly seductive but she exerted her will and didn't lift her arms in a protective gesture. It was disgust that sent the sudden tremor through her, she told herself firmly; any other explanation was unthinkable!

'My sisterly loyalty doesn't extend that far,' she sneered. 'As you're so interested, you were never meant to know I wasn't Elizabeth. Whatever qualms I might have had about the morality of my sister's scheme vanished about three seconds after I met you,' she confided hotly. 'If any man deserves to be left at the altar you do!' she cried recklessly. 'All you care about is your inflated ego and power.'

It did occur to her as she subsided, her breath coming fast and uneven, that she wasn't exactly being wise in taking such a provocative line. What had Elizabeth said? 'You don't know Morgan. He's capable of anything. He'll do something to split us up...hurt Bill. He's obsessed with staying in control of the company; he has to marry someone, and time's running out. Besides, you don't jilt an Urquart, Rosie!'

Had she really thought Elizabeth was being pointlessly vindictive? A bubble of hysterical mirth at her recollection struggled to escape her dry throat. 'I realise you might be a little annoyed,' she observed placatingly.

'"A little annoyed".' He repeated the words slowly, his sardonic smile calculatingly increasing the tension which she could almost see around them, crackling like blue fire. 'How astute,' he breathed, and the low tone of his vibrant voice made something inside her snap.

'That's it!' she bit out. 'Enough of the long-drawn-out pauses and sinister hints. You're madder than hell that Elizabeth tricked you. When I met you and saw first-hand what a cold, callous, egotistical swine you actually are, I'd have done anything to help Elizabeth slip through your fingers.'

She made a scornful noise and placed her hands akimbo on her hips, causing the shimmering fabric to pull taut across her breasts, emphasising the heaving contours.

'Gunther tells me you're some sort of genius,' she continued with withering scorn. 'He could be right, but you're a pretty poor judge of character if you thought Elizabeth would ever be satisfied with being the dutiful and decorative wife, with an acceptable genetic pool and good, child-bearing hips.

'Elizabeth is a creature of impulse. She agreed to marry you because she was flattered and the man she loved had slipped out of her life. She wanted to punish him, and please our father's social ambitions. She'd never have married you; she's mercurial, not mad! I was a diversion—not good but adequate, or so I thought. If she hadn't been so scared of telling you the truth none of this would have occurred in the first place,' she pointed out. 'You bullied her.'

The fury that had exploded in her like a Roman candle had just about burnt itself out; she felt drained and suddenly cold. 'What can I say? This wasn't the wisest acquisition you ever made, or rather didn't make,' she said sombrely.

'Oh, but I purchased in good faith.' His expression, for him, was curiously revealing. It was equally divided between repugnance and fascination; but Rosie, unable to withstand his dissecting regard, fixed her eyes on a dark point over his shoulder.

The difference between her and her twin could never have been more obvious. No doubt he found her twin's smooth, conciliatory manner much more appealing than her own rash hostility. 'Try purring instead of scratching, Rosie; it's so much more productive,' her twin had safely advised her on more than one occasion.

'You can't purchase a wife!' She would never purr with this man, she decided, her chin rising to a belligerent angle.

He gave a minute grimace which managed to convey impatience and scorn at her words. 'I need a wife; your sister knew this; she knew I had invested time in selecting someone not averse to the arrangement. I have a time limit.

I went to great lengths to avoid all this emotional melodrama, only to find myself lumbered with a female who appears to permanently hover on the border of hysteria.'

She dismissed this claim with a caustic twist of her lips. 'I don't care about you or your time limits.' He couldn't be suggesting what she thought he was; not even Morgan Urquart could suggest something that preposterous!

'Well, you should, because they are going to affect your future.' His voice had a rich, satiny, gloating quality.

'Get to the point. What exactly are you trying to say?' The sooner she was out of this place, this country, and back to the hectic sanity of her normal life, the better.

'I need a wife—and, as Elizabeth is already spoken for, you'll have to do.'

She stared at him, not trusting the evidence of her own ears. 'You're insane,' she said with deep conviction, her golden eyes glowing with scorn. 'I have an allergy to marriage in general, but to you...! Tell me, Morgan, what possible reason would I have for obliging you? I hear from everyone about your incredible intellect, but so far you've just acted like your common-or-garden conceited, puffed-up megalomaniac! Go and marry that silly child who thinks you're God's gift,' she advised scornfully.

'I have no wish to ruin Ellie's life.'

'Mine isn't up for grabs either,' she stated drily.

'You're the one who offered herself up as a substitute,' he reminded her grimly. 'I worked hard to pull the family company into the twentieth century. It had been brought to a sorry state by a group of people who put their own vanity and self-interest above common sense. The old man knew that when he was too frail to hold the reins they'd tear the heart from what he'd built up, and he let them, the idea being that I wouldn't be able to resist the urge to prevent them destroying his lifetime's work. He was a gambler.'

A definite gleam of appreciation illuminated the depths of his metallic eyes as they skimmed over her. He seemed satisfied that he had her full attention. 'He wanted to show me that when the chips were down this was where I belonged. He also knew I wouldn't let the pack back in to dabble disastrously with the livelihood of several hundred people. This last manipulation was his way of definitely ensuring the line of succession.

'He knew I had no intention of marrying,' he added drily. 'But in this day and age,' he continued, scorn leavening his voice, 'and in a competitive field, there is no place for amateurs, even talented ones, and the members of my family involved don't even have that going for them. If marriage is the only way I'll keep them at bay, so be it. You will marry me. I won't be cheated.'

At least his words held a ring of sincerity, but they also revealed his apparently limitless belief in his own ability, and carried a definite threat, implicit in every impassioned syllable. 'I can hardly be held responsible for the vagaries of your grandfather's will.' Surely he didn't think she was insane enough to even listen to his ridiculous suggestion? No, she mentally corrected, not a suggestion—more of a royal decree.

'I was prepared to sacrifice my freedom to some extent and make the fine adjustment necessary.'

'Is applause expected at this point?' He made marriage sound childishly, ridiculously simple. The look he cast in her direction made her bite her unruly tongue. 'Be realistic, Morgan. You have a lot to gain from marrying, but my sister had precious little and I have nothing,' she said bluntly, holding both hands palm upwards and attempting a conciliatory smile. But any diplomat would have been disappointed at the effort; it carried no conviction.

His smile had a silky quality that she was already beginning to associate with danger. 'So that's it, is it? You and your twin have had a good laugh at my expense. It must have been a thrilling little game—some compensation for all the mischievous tricks you missed out on as children.

But you're not a child now.' His voice grated harshly across her nerve-endings and she shivered. 'You're an adult who should expect to pay the consequences of her actions. Albeit a shallow—'

'Shallow!' she breathed wrathfully. This man was beyond belief. '*You* were about to buy a bride!'

'An agreement was reached and a bargain struck, and you appear to be thinking of reneging.' He shook his head slowly. 'Don't even consider it.' His words had the velocity of a gunshot blast and she swayed as if caught in a violent storm.

'Your arrangement was with Elizabeth,' she protested, watching him move from the outer side of the work counter with dismay; humouring lunatics was not really her forte.

'You were quite happy to substitute for her earlier.' His smile was slow, sensual, and this sudden change of attack made her breathless. The harsh lines on his face deepened with fastidious distaste as he moved to within a foot of her. As she raised her head she realised how intimidating his height could be under certain circumstances. He carried those extra inches easily, with casual grace.

'I chose your sister because I had no intention of making major adaptations to my life in order to accommodate a wife and family. I didn't want to inflict unnecessary harm on some idealistic female who imagined she could alter me to fit into some cosy dream,' he told her scornfully.

'I don't require or desire love!'

His lip curled in open contempt. 'I thought your sister was ideal—experienced enough to have left romantic illusion behind. In fact she was presentable, but superficial—the ideal combination. She certainly raised no objections, whatever she might have told you. In fact she seemed positively eager.'

'Elizabeth seems lots of things she isn't,' Rosie told him hoarsely. If their places had been reversed, and it had been she who had been billeted with her father, would she have been like Elizabeth, attention-seeking to compensate for the lack of genuine affection she'd been shown at home, rejected by her mother? As always she felt the familiar surge of guilt and protectiveness. Morgan's cold-blooded complacence filled her with stunned disbelief; this monster gave the word cynical a whole new meaning!

'I am no longer interested in your sister.'

'I think you are; she's made you look foolish and you can't take that; you're interested in revenge. Call me a taxi; I've had enough of this. I'm going home.'

He caught her by the shoulders firmly enough to draw a grunt of pain from her throat. The dilation of her pupils was the only concession she made to fear.

'Let me go...!' she spat in a furious tone.

'How much do you care for your sister?'

'I doubt if you're equipped to understand, so I won't bore you with the details.' He had bent closer, his head inclined intimidatingly close. She could see the close-pored texture of his skin, the small scar that ran down the length of his jaw—a white, almost invisible thread—and the shape of his lips... She blinked hard to dispel the strange confusion which seemed to be seeping into her brain.

'How would your sister cope with a husband who was unemployed, and unemployable?' he asked thoughtfully, as though the idea held appeal to him.

She froze, colour seeping from her face. 'Bill has a job; he's an electronics engineer. He has an excellent post in California; you can't do anything to him.' The uncertainty that had crept into her voice was dismaying, especially as he couldn't have failed to hear the crumbling of defiance in the quavering tone. A sick feeling was growing in her belly.

Returning the glimmering stare of her adversary with stoical stubbornness, she realised why her sister had only imagined herself safe from retribution if the Atlantic separated her and her estranged fiancé. Could it be that even that wasn't a safe distance?

'You may or may not be aware that I had and still retain connections in the States. In fact, the owner of the company dear Bill has gone to work for is a friend of mine.'

'Male bonding—how touching,' she observed with sweet venom. A true son of Machiavelli, she thought bitterly as sweat broke out on her pale brow.

'To be frank, I was instrumental in getting him the post.'

'I'll take it as read, shall I, that you weren't motivated by natural generosity?'

He regarded her as though she'd made a fatuous remark not worthy of his notice. 'I decided I'd feel more confident of Elizabeth's short-term fidelity if he was out of sight.' He gave an infinitesimal shrug and loosened the hold on her upper arms. He looked at the visible marks on her fair skin and his hands fell away. Was his frown self-critical? She could hardly believe so.

'So much for your precautions.' The calculating way he ran his life deeply offended her; everything about him was anathema to her. Moreover, the awful certainty that she too was being manipulated was growing with each passing second; she didn't want to listen to any more but a perverse curiosity made her wait for him to continue.

'But it's so convenient now if I want to alter his employment status. Just a phone call away. I call in a favour; it's that simple.'

The blatant threat made her grow deathly pale and, objectively watching her response with grim satisfaction, Morgan wondered if she was going to faint. But no, she had spirit; he had to admit that.

'You would do that?' The scorn in her voice for some reason made him angry—almost as angry as he'd felt the moment he'd realised the deception being carried out for his benefit.

'One word from me and Bill will never work in the industry again. I can't see that leading to domestic harmony, can you?'

'That is despicable,' she said, her voice low and throbbing with contempt. She pressed her fingers to her temple where the pounding pulse made her feel as though her head was about to explode. 'It's blackmail!'

'The stakes are high; if you're squeamish it's best not to get involved. But you got involved, didn't you?' he said cuttingly. 'I imagine you thought it was amusing.' His eyes were drawn to her high, full breasts thrust against the thin fabric as she raised her arms. Eyes glittering, his chin jerked upwards as though struck by some invisible hand. 'It's time to find out just what priority you do place on your twin's happiness.'

A voice that rich, she thought, should have been warm; his was as cold and hard as a shower of hail. 'You're a shallow, pleasure-seeking little tramp, but it seems to me you have one weakness, and that's your sister. That's why I think you'll marry me, Rosie.'

'I have a life of my own, a job, my mother needs me.' She had to make him see that what he was suggesting was insane, unacceptable. 'Two days out of your life; that's all I'm asking, Rosie.' The words came back to haunt her. 'It's just a precaution.' Why was she pleading? she thought angrily. She should be pummelling his smug face with her fists.

'I'm sure you have a deeply fulfilling role basking in the reflected glory of your parent, but I doubt very much if you're indispensible. It must be frustrating for the untalented to be around the inspired, but they do congregate. It seems to me that your life is the glamorous version of staying home to look after the sick parent...lack of guts passing for devotion.'

'You overbearing, smug bastard! I couldn't understand why Elizabeth was so convinced you'd react vindictively if she thwarted you, but she was right to be afraid, wasn't she? You haven't a scrap of common decency in your body. To ruin two people's lives just to stay on top of the heap is disgusting.' She was shaking, and tears of fury clouded her vision. She struck out blindly. He fielded the assault with dismissive ease and exerted enough force to send her panting against the hard, solid length of him.

Being bombarded with alien and disruptive sensations was the last thing she needed at that particular moment. Choice, however, didn't enter into the way she was painfully aware of the thud of his heart confined in the vault of his deeply muscled chest. Lean, whipcord strength was apparent as he casually subdued her reactionary struggle. A humiliating lassitude began to steal over her without warning. Fiercely she tried to subdue her consciousness of the male smell that rose from his warm skin.

'I'll take that as a yes, shall I?' he said, pushing his fingers into the lush mass of her raven-dark hair and exerting enough pressure to pull her head backwards, whilst his other arm in the small of her back kept her firmly and distressingly plastered against him.

'Don't rely on my suicidal instincts; I have none.'

The deep laughter that vibrated in his chest emerged warm and spontaneous, lacking his habitual cynical jaundice. 'I beg to differ. I'd say that's exactly what you *do* have if you willingly went along with your sister's scheme. Or *was* it her scheme? Maybe you're bored with running around after a spoilt celebrity. Did the idea of a rich husband seem too good an opportunity to pass up?' His lips curled cynically.

The laughter made her freeze in total amazement; his smile had a voltage off the scale. Was this the Urquart charm Elizabeth had mentioned? She suddenly felt absurdly piqued that he had smiled at Elizabeth like that. Then his sneering afterthought made her eyes flash. 'You really do love yourself, don't you? I...I...' She began to stutter as her righteous indignation threatened to overcome her.

He gave another rumble of laughter as she stamped her foot in inarticulate rage. Then the humour died abruptly from his face, to be instantly replaced by a fierce, predatory expression. Hypnotic, luminous eyes ran compulsively over her face and lower. The hand that had been entangled deep in her hair moved to stroke the elegant line of her throat from jaw to shoulderblade; it made her quiver like a finely tuned, sensitive violin string.

He was going to kiss her, she realised at that point, and strangely she wasn't trying to avoid it; and the intimate scrutiny which ought to have repelled her just made the pit of her belly disintegrate into a warm, liquid emptiness.

His tongue slid between her lips and there was no barrier to prevent it. Her entire being was concentrated on the sensation and taste of his mouth—a subtle and skilful mouth that was eliciting a slow-burning response inside her. At what point she began to return the pressure, and passivity was transformed into eager, almost violent responsiveness, she never worked out.

She registered the hungry, rampant expression in his eyes in some corner of her mind that was still independently functioning, and she felt as well as heard the guttural sound of male satisfaction that was ripped from his throat. None of this was anything more than further impetus to press closer, to sink into the abyss of dark, delicious sensations. She trembled on the brink as he slid his hand under the shoulder of her dress, pushing back the fabric to reveal the flawless curve of her shoulder.

She shuddered as his lips touched the exposed skin. The pagan lick of desire slid like wildfire through her veins, the terrible, marvellous hunger all-consuming; her fingers, clumsy but eager, reached for him, delighted in the tactile sensations. Her breath came in small, uneven gasps.

He watched her face through the shield of thick dark lashes that shaded his own half-closed eyes. 'Being married to me might have its compensations,' he mused throatily, and his tongue traced a line to the pulse at the base of her neck. 'Strange… You look identical to your sister, but whilst I found her beautiful I never felt any urge to strangle her, or this equally compelling urge to tear off her clothes and make love to her on the carpet.'

Whatever insanity had held her in its thrall, his words loosened the hold, and with a gasp of self-disgust she pulled free. 'Don't flatter yourself,' she hissed. What had she done? she wondered despairingly. His shirt was completely adrift from the waistband of his trousers and his jacket was over on the other side of the room, lying in a crumpled heap on the floor.

Her stomach muscles clenched as her eyes followed the light sprinkling of hair that covered his chest and ran in a darting line down his flat belly to disappear from view. His skin had a satiny quality, she recalled, and something twisted inside her, as sharp and vicious as a slicing blade, as he shifted his position and the muscles moved fluidly beneath his skin—smooth, not bulky, yet clearly delineated.

'Nothing in this world could compensate me for that—certainly not a few kisses,' she said derisively, tearing her eyes clear of his torso. 'Don't delude yourself.'

His narrowed eyes moved from the erratic pulse throbbing in her neck to the faint sheen of perspiration that gave a faint glow to her skin, and the tenor of his uneven breathing slowed. 'If you're trying to tell me you didn't enjoy that, I'd say it's you who's hooked on delusion.'

He gave a dismissive shrug and began to button his shirt with economical movements that betrayed none of the trembling uncertainty that incapacitated her own limbs. 'As you're the mother of my future children I'd say a mutual physical attraction is a plus factor.' He ran a hand through his disordered hair, and Rosie recalled her fingers diving into the lush thickness with a dull disbelief. A fresh rush of blood sent heat through her body.

'Elizabeth was so right to believe you have no scruples.

Would you really ruin the life of a man who has done you no harm? Don't you feel any remorse when you resort to blackmail? Or is this sort of behaviour an everyday occurrence for you?' Her eyes searched his face, hoping to find some remorse—anything to allow her to believe that his threats were empty. She'd never met Bill but he'd always sounded almost *too* nice for her sister. But Morgan didn't care whether he was nice or not; everyone was fair game for his manipulations.

'It's what you believe I'll do that matters,' he observed, and there was no hint of softness in his expression. 'Don't look so tragic, Rosie; you might even find you enjoy yourself.' His cynicism was laced with a degree of sensuality that made her skin grow hot.

She hated his reference to the fact that she'd behaved in a disgraceful and humiliating fashion, like some sex-starved idiot.

'You have to take into account the fact that earlier this evening I had to leave Gunther much sooner than I'd have liked.' She pouted provocatively and silently praised her own ingenuity. 'I think you could term it extenuating circumstances. I wouldn't like to foster false expectations.'

The lines around Morgan's mouth grew more deeply pronounced and something akin to anger flared in his eyes. The ultimate egotist would react badly to being considered a substitute, she decided complacently.

'And was Gunther in on your scam?'

Rosie let the threatening tone glance off her oversensitive skin. Gunther, at least, could watch his own back; it was so pleasant not to feel responsible for someone. Though whether he would approve of her small, face-saving deceit was another matter. 'He wasn't happy, under the circumstances,' she said with no word of a lie.

'He must be a very tolerant lover.'

Rosie's smile held a hint of affectionate contrition. 'He is.'

'Was.' His glance was steely and as uncompromising as the line of his lips.

'Threats follow blackmail like night after day,' she said with a show of dismissive unconcern. Inside she seethed with rebellion; he'd cornered and coerced her, but inside she'd never submit. What was that old saying about prisons and bars? she wondered. 'I thought the arrangement I inherited included a carte blanche to do our own thing?'

She wrapped her arms around her aching breasts, which remained a very visible reminder of her recent arousal, and the way his eyes intermittently drifted in that direction was becoming difficult to cope with. 'You can't change all the rules. You might be able to blackmail me into marrying you but don't expect me to enjoy the experience.'

'My arrangement with your sister is no longer relevant.'

His unhelpful response filled her with frustrated anger. 'You might as well tell me what the house rules are to be so that I can be sure to break them!' she returned sarcastically.

'It would make sense to begin our family swiftly, and I'd like to be certain of the pedigree of any progeny.'

She gasped in outrage at the calm insult. 'This has only just occurred to you?' The bed-hopping bimbo, that's me, she thought with grim self-derision. He really did have a fine opinion of her character.

'Unlike Elizabeth, who is vain and imagines no man can see the deceit beyond the empty promises, you are motivated by a passionate nature; this makes you a more volatile proposition. You've proved that you don't think before you act,' he said, his voice harsh. 'Your mother's exploits are fairly well documented and to expect you not to have been tainted by the eccentric lifestyle you have been raised to consider normal would be unreasonable. You're a passionate woman to whom casual liaisons are the norm.'

He shrugged his magnificent shoulders in a manner that expressed mild contempt. 'That's fine whilst you are Rosie

Osborne, but not when you're an Urquart. Your sister has a finesse and discretion you totally lack. So for the present you will curtail your involvements with other men.'

'You think so?' she responded, the sudden increase in her pulse rate sending hot colour to stain the curve of her high cheekbones a deep carnation-pink. His reputation as a connoisseur of beautiful women made his contemptuous observation the height of hypocrisy. It was partly this unsavoury side of his nature that had made Rosie agree to this charade to begin with. Elizabeth had been very graphic in her descriptions. 'But considering my complete lack of morals, aren't you taking an enormous chance?' she sneered.

'Thanks to you and your sister, I'm constrained. I would hardly have chosen you as a wife if I had alternatives—'

'Don't take that high moral tone with me!' she interrupted, punctuating each word with a vicious blow to the oak panelling beside her. It occurred to her that her behaviour was reinforcing his completely unique view of her as a wild, passionate, unpredictable siren. She, Rosie, pragmatic to the core! 'I'm the one being constrained here and I'll never forget it. Morals didn't stop you wanting to rip my clothes off!' Or anyone else's that strikes your fancy, she thought bitterly. She blushed scarlet and desperately wished she'd kept the lid on that particular pot.

'Did I say that?' One darkly delineated brow rose. 'How crude and indelicate of me,' he said, a smile, a very disturbing smile, playing about the corners of his mouth. 'Actually I'd much prefer to remove your clothes...very slowly.' His thick dark lashes flickered against his cheek as his glance travelled slowly over her lightly clad frame.

Angry coherence dissolved into total confusion under the speculative gleam in his unfathomable eyes... Would she always feel so exposed, so vulnerable when he chose to blatantly display the devastating sexuality that was the most confusing component of his complex personality? The words...his voice...were wildly erotic, and her body's mindless response made her want to scream in despair.

'You think I'm influenced in my demands by the fact that I want to sleep with you,' he said mildly. 'Forget that possibility, my dear; I never confuse business with pleasure. Marriage would hardly be a prerequisite to enjoying your favours.' His open contempt made her feel unclean. 'I'm no jealous lover, Rosie, just a man who wants to guard his investment. I have no desire for a promiscuous wife.' The last comment held a note of silky menace.

'I have no desire for a husband. And if you want a wife who loathes you you must be unhinged.'

'Sacrifice is character-building,' he said austerely. 'We can both discover the truth of that pearl of wisdom.'

'Your precious company means more to you than anything!' she accused, swallowing the tears of self-pity that welled up; Urquarts probably didn't cry either, she thought derisively. 'People are just pawns to you.'

He looked slightly bored by this accusation. 'This is one game I didn't invite you to join, but now you have you'll play according to my rules.'

'Bill didn't ask to play your sick games but you're happy to ruin his life, so don't try and make yourself sound reasonable,' she said contemptuously. 'What happens if I don't stick to your rules?' she then asked jauntily. But her defiance was all superficial and he probably knew it.

His smile was lethal and very civilised; it made the blood chill in her veins. 'I don't think that's a possibility you should dwell on, my dear.'

'I want to go home. I'm cold and I've no intention of spending the night with you.'

'How delightfully old-fashioned of you, darling, not to want to anticipate the marriage vows. Strange, but I construed your earlier...enthusiasm as meaning something quite different.'

'Cut out the sarcasm and take me home.' She didn't need

the reminder; how could she forget the explosive reaction his caress had generated?

Surprisingly, after a short and intense scrutiny of her upturned pale face, he nodded a curt assent. 'I have a meeting first thing. Besides, I have to deal with my family—and you had better inform your father that he has had the wrong daughter under his roof for the past few days.'

'He'll never accept my marrying you.' Filled with fresh despair, and taking on board part of the full implication of the situation she had got herself into, she lowered her head, sending a shimmering curtain of hair around her face.

He took her arm, smiling thinly as she flinched, and led her to the front door. 'I take it you don't want to stop for coffee,' he observed drily. 'And by the way, I think making it a love match with your sister tactfully stepping aside would be a suitable pose to adopt.'

She stopped dead and stared at him, transfixed. 'Are you going to say that?'

'I have no intention of offering anyone any explanations,' he said in a tone of mild surprise.

Rosie gave a dry laugh. 'Silly me. Do you walk on water too?' she enquired pleasantly from between gritted teeth.

'Facetiousness is so unattractive in a woman,' he observed, reactivating the alarm system before closing the door.

'And smug superiority is unattractive in a man,' she muttered beneath her breath as she followed him to the car.

'There's a rug in the back seat if you're cold,' he said as she buckled her belt swiftly, wanting no repeat of the previous occasion. Her eagerness was observed with a faint derisory glance as he interpreted its cause correctly.

'Your concern for my welfare is heart-warming,' she said, reaching for the rug and pulling the wool fabric around her shoulders.

'A bride with a red nose would look all wrong in the society pages,' he observed drily, and she glared at him with venom and retreated beneath the voluminous folds.

CHAPTER FOUR

ROSIE CROUCHED AT THE TOP of the stairs, listening to her father's hearty attempts at conversation with Morgan—the man who was to become her husband the following morning. The idea still seemed too bizarre to be real.

'I'm sure she won't be long.'

Rosie smiled complacently. Was half an hour long enough, she wondered, to keep her suitor waiting? Five more minutes might just do it. Listening to her father's obsequious efforts was making her more uncomfortable than the cramp in her left foot—the result of the awkward position she was adopting.

It was amazing, she reflected bleakly, the way her parents had reacted differently to her news. Her father had adapted with remarkable ease to the situation; any link, it seemed, to an Urquart was better than none from his point of view. It was a philosophy she found herself despising. At least her mother was honest—totally concerned with how this situation would inconvenience herself, but honest about it. 'I do think you're being remarkably selfish, darling.'

After enduring a half-hour lecture this had been the final straw. Rosie had laughed until the tears had rolled down her cheeks. Unable to explain the irony to her mother, she had hung up the phone in despair.

'I think I'll go and hurry Rosie along.'

Rosie got to her feet hurriedly as this last comment drifted up the staircase. Chin held high, she began her descent. Her mother was big on entrances, so she was emulating the expert—at least to a point. Beatrice Lane was a valued client of a handful of fashion houses and Rosie's present outfit had lots of labels, but none of them exclusive.

Her father's reaction was all she'd hoped for: he changed colour, becoming a violent shade of purple, and made a choking noise in his throat. As Rosie reached the foot of the staircase he looked with foreboding at the tall man beside him. A public demonstration of Morgan's horror had been too much to hope for, Rosie realised, venturing a brief glimpse in that direction herself. But if her present get-up wasn't enough to make him furious, nothing would.

He was hiding it well, though, she had to admit. She had imagined he would look good in formal dress, but in the flesh words were insufficient to describe him. He was, simply, magnificent! She felt the air escape her lungs in one smothered gasp; the magnetism he radiated was too potent to take in.

'Sorry I'm late,' she said airily, bestowing a generous smile on the two men and avoiding direct eye contact with the younger.

'Not at all, Rosie; I can see you've put a *great* deal of effort into getting ready.' Morgan sounded remarkably comfortable, she realised, with a situation that had been meant to reduce him to incoherent rage. The beginnings of a frown tugged at her dark, well-defined brows.

'I put a great deal of thought into it,' she agreed. Her long, beaded earrings swung against her cheek as she spoke and he actually grinned when she winced as one swung into her eye.

'Eye-catching in every sense of the word,' he observed silkily.

'You can't go like that.' Her father had recovered his voice but his colour remained alarmingly high, and Rosie hoped, with a spasm of guilt, she hadn't done anything too drastic to his blood pressure.

'Is something wrong with it?' she enquired with a puzzled frown. She glanced down at herself. The correct effect had been tough to achieve; she'd been aiming at a bohemian look—in a gaudy, tacky sort of way. The flea market had been invaluable in her frenzied search to achieve it. The exotic cast of her features and her dark colouring had produced an unexpectedly gypsyish appearance.

The layered, swirling skirts, which clashed quite gloriously, were topped by several shirts and a patchwork waistcoat. The boots were so sturdy that they felt like lead weights around her ankles; even allowing for the peculiarities of fashion trends, they had never been meant for a drawing room! Rosie, more used to casual, uncluttered tailoring, thought she looked like a freak. But it should give the precious Urquarts something to think about. The daughter-in-law from hell was out to make an impact.

'Donald, you must allow for individual expression.'

Her father looked almost as flabbergasted by this statement as Rosie felt. He looked around, unsure of the safest response, but was congenitally incapable of contradicting the younger man. Did anyone ever challenge Morgan's casual assumption of command? she wondered bitterly. This intrinsic air of authority made her want to scream. If she told her father that Morgan was blackmailing her into marriage he would probably feign deafness, she decided bitterly.

'If you don't like what I'm wearing, Father, say so,' she bit out. 'You don't have to allow *him* to tell you what to think.' She cast Morgan a fulminating look full of loathing. The target of her strategy had turned out to be totally immune to her tactics and she wanted to throttle him. Moments before she had felt like a crusading rebel—and now she felt shabby and foolish, standing there in all that garish trash.

'Don't speak to your father in that tone.'

She swung back towards Morgan, her bosom heaving dramatically, causing the numerous beads she was wearing to jingle gently. 'I don't need your advice on good manners.'

Morgan cast her a slow, considering look and his expression was as uncompromising as granite, but less roughly hewn. His skin was tawny and had the glow of health and his hair was burnished a few shades lighter. His profile was enough to inspire any sculpture, but could any artist capture the essence of vitality that this man exuded? She doubted it. Just looking at him made her feel light-headed.

'Donald, you go on ahead and make our apologies. Give us thirty minutes. Tell the driver I shan't be needing him.' The smile was smooth, almost conspiratorial, and she watched her father do as he was bid like some obedient poodle.

'I've no intention of changing,' she announced as silence returned once the door closed. 'If your blue-blooded family don't like me...' Her shoulders shrugged expressively.

'I think it was unkind of you to embarrass your father.'

This soft comment sent colour flooding into her face. 'How fortunate I don't give a damn what you think. It seems to me that people worry far too much about your opinion.'

He accepted her retort with nothing more than a thin-lipped smile. 'I can appreciate that you put considerable time and effort into proving how unsuitable a wife you would make—a wasted effort because I already know that. I believe they call it Hobson's choice, and the sooner you accept that the better. If it makes you any happier I am hardly ecstatic with the arrangement either. Neither do I embarrass easily, so all this...' he caught a trailing gauzy scarf that she had wrapped around her head '...is quite wasted. Aren't you a little...mature to be a rebel?'

'I suppose you're not going to persuade me to dress in a more dignified manner,' she said scornfully. 'Why else did you send my father on ahead?'

'The poor man looked apoplectic,' he observed drily. 'And I feel I should support your effort at informality. I have every intention that you should attend this event looking as you intended.'

'Support…?' she said suspiciously. The triumph she had anticipated earlier was never going to materialise and she gloomily accepted that fact.

'I can hardly appear with such a vision on my arm dressed like this.' He touched the pristine whiteness of his shirt-front. 'We must present a picture of solidarity.'

Baffled, she stared at him as he rang for a cab.

The journey to his home took five minutes, and was accomplished in silence. A silence which gave her ample time to surmise wildly about what he had in mind when he spoke of solidarity.

He unlocked the front door and, holding her firmly by the arm, began to climb the staircase, his long legs taking them two at a time.

'What will the servants think if they see you dragging me upstairs?'

'I don't encourage anyone to wait up for me. I'm capable of undressing myself, unless there are any better offers.'

She gave a snort of disgust as he gave her a speculative leer. 'Slow down,' she panted, and the colour in her cheeks wasn't solely attributable to the hectic ascent.

'We're almost there, darling,' he said unsympathetically, the endearment silkily sarcastic on his tongue. He opened a door with a flourish and thrust her inside.

'This is your bedroom,' she accused, looking around the large room as he closed the door firmly behind her. The mainly antique furniture and oak-panelled walls made little impact, beyond a vague impression of masculine utility; luxuriously spartan, was the phrase that briefly flew into her head as she took in her surroundings.

'*Our* bedroom in the near future.'

'There's still time…'

He gave a dry laugh. 'For me to change mind? I think not.' His tie was flung onto the bed and he began to unbutton his shirt.

'What do you think you're doing?' she said, her eyes wide as the shirt followed the tie.

'Taking off my clothes. You can avert your gaze if it offends your maidenly eyes.'

Would it were that easy! His skin was tanned an even deep gold, and as he half turned she watched, with fascination, the muscles of his shoulders ripple. 'If you lay a finger on me…'

He paused in the act of unzipping his trousers and turned to give her a scornfully ironic stare. 'My dear girl, it would take at least half an hour to unpeel your layers and my mother has a fetish concerning punctuality.'

'And you always please Mummy.'

'Rarely, if she is to be believed.' He gave a faint half-smile and his eyes touched her tense face. The grey was tinged with a perceptible smokiness that matched the slight rasp in his voice when he spoke again. 'I don't see any point in needlessly aggravating her but I don't cringe from it when I deem it necessary. You seem piqued that I'm not attempting to seduce you.'

She injected as much scorn as she could muster into her laugh. 'It seems to me that the love affair you have with yourself precludes any other involvement.' Was he suggesting that the present situation was sufficiently important for him to 'deem it necessary' to annoy his mother?

The dark trousers joined the rest of his clothes and she swallowed the painful, aching constriction in her throat. He had the body of an athlete at the height of his power. Considering the fact that from an early age she had sat and watched her mother paint live nude models, she couldn't comprehend the surge of response that rose inside her like a tidal wave. There was nothing aesthetic in her appreciation of his masculine beauty…it was earthier…more visceral.

He gave a sudden laugh. 'Narcissistic?' He considered this viewpoint with open amusement. 'I've never been accused of that before.'

'People are too busy grovelling. I expect you're surrounded by yes-men.' Her eyes widened as he pulled on a pair of jeans with a jagged tear in one knee.

He buckled his belt across his lean waist and selected a T-shirt from a drawer. 'My grandfather's mistake was being the complete despot; I, on the other hand, stifle any natural inclinations I have in that direction.' A dark brow shot up. 'I see you look skeptical, but behaving the way he did displays poor business sense. The old man never delegated or gave responsibility—which is fine in the short term.'

His voice became muffled as he pulled the black cotton over his head. 'Problem is, minus the despot the structure crumbles, because no one knows how to think. I like people around me who can function independently and aren't afraid to tell me I'm wrong. I don't give house room to boot-lickers. These, I think.'

He held out a pair of boots for her inspection. They were tan leather and looked like something a cowboy might wear. 'Have you ever ridden in the States, Rosie?' He straightened up and ran his fingers through his tousled hair. The transformation from his austere beauty in formal dress to casual and slightly dangerous informality was fascinating to watch. Two different men, and both extremely fascinating. Will the real Morgan Urquart stand up? she thought whimsically.

'I don't ride.'

'The saddles are armchairs there. Perhaps I'll take you one day.'

'What are you doing, Morgan?' she asked with a hint of weariness. He had a disturbing habit of taking the initiative away from her.

'Dressing for dinner, what else?'

'Like that?'

'I've no beads, unless you lend me some of those.'

She had never actually imagined he'd let her go to the dinner party dressed like a reject from a charity shop. She had made a great show of flouting conventionality but had never expected to be permitted, let alone encouraged, to go through with it. 'What would your mother say if you turned up like that?'

'Quite a lot, I would think,' he observed cheerfully.

'You can't expect me to face your family like this,' she said with dawning horror. Her brilliant theories were dying a violent death as she imagined herself surrounded by glittering, patrician critics.

'Wasn't that the idea?' The taunt was soft and accurately targeted. 'Or did you have ideas of me forcibly undressing you?'

'Certainly not,' she denied, with a haste that gave her words a curious lack of sincerity; her confusion and dismay were increasing by leaps and bounds. The series of vivid and shocking images that were instigated by his taunt were frighteningly seductive; what was happening to her?

'I would have appreciated a choice, not a phone call from your PA instructing me to be ready,' she snapped, her voice as brittle as glass. 'I have no wish to be paraded before your family like some piece of breeding stock. I don't care if they like me. You don't; why should they be different?'

He levered himself from the mantelpiece he'd been propped up against and took her by the chin, his fingers along the line of her jaw resisting her attempts to look elsewhere than at his face. 'You sound as if you want me to,' he observed huskily, his contemplative grin widening as her eyes grew round with outrage. 'If that is the case perhaps you should put some effort into making yourself agreeable.'

'Dream on,' she replied huskily as several hundred emotions clawed and fought inside her.

The pause whilst his glittering eyes bored into her was painful. 'From my point of view it's equally irrelevant as to whether my family like you or you like me,' he drawled. 'One of us is lying; I wonder which one?' His thumb stroked her cheek carelessly; she doubted if he was aware of it. It brought a flood of debilitating heat to her lower body and she felt intensely ashamed of the unbidden response.

'You wanted to aggravate me and it backfired,' he went on. 'So you'll just have to grit your teeth and bluff it out. Never play poker if you're not prepared to have your bluff called,' he advised. 'I'm not a person who has ever felt constrained by the narrow bounds of social conformity, Rosie.'

'Grit my teeth and bluff it out,' she echoed. 'Sounds like a recipe for our marriage.' He certainly wasn't part of the herd, she was forced to agree.

'You're asking to have your bluff called once more, Rosie,' he said, his fingers sliding into her hair against her scalp. 'Whilst our marriage is one of convenience…'

'Whose convenience?' she muttered truculently, her sense of injustice rising at approximately the same rate as her panic. The havoc his touch was wreaking on her nervous system—an almost impersonal, careless touch—was appalling. She felt like a mass of indiscriminate cravings.

'Physically at least there is something,' he observed, as if he was attuned to her turbulent emotions. His eyes half closed over the glittering gleam of his disruptive gaze as they fell to her lips, which were full, soft, pink and quivering.

She began to shake her head in frenzied denial. But the kiss he bestowed on her was a devastating way of making a nonsense of that denial. The masculine essence of him was like a heady drug, and when he broke away she knew that the soft cry of protest emerged from her own swollen lips. 'I'd call that something...' he said throatily, and his eyes on her face glittered with a banked-down fever.

Taking deep draughts of air to replenish her starved lungs, Rosie pulled free of the insidiously unsettling contact. 'All that proves is that you're a competent kisser,' she retorted shakily. Pull yourself together, Rosie, girl, she chided herself. 'I've no doubt you've had plenty of practice.' The last words emerged as a sneer. She could still taste him, and she rubbed her mouth as if to wipe away the flavour, all her senses heightened to a painful degree.

'You sound an authority on the subject,' he said with a quirk of one eyebrow.

'It's common knowledge,' she responded. 'Besides, Elizabeth said...'

'Go on; what did Elizabeth say?'

Rosie drew a deep, angry breath; how dared he look amused? 'I suppose you're proud of your reputation as some sort of stud,' she jeered.

'I don't know what your sister has been telling you but I guard my private life with a zeal some consider obsessive.'

'Why would Elizabeth lie...?' she began, her voice openly sceptical. Then a reason presented itself—a very possible reason for misrepresentation. Her twin had known she would be far more likely to be co-operative if the man she was anxious to escape from was a moral degenerate. 'I suppose you're some sort of saint,' she snapped, working hard to keep her dismay out of her voice.

'That would be stretching credibility,' he conceded. 'I don't aspire to celibacy. But my relationships with women have never relied on deceit. Mind you, some women find the truth less than comfortable,' he observed with an air of weary cynicism.

'That sounds ruthless.' The words slipped out of their own volition, her eyes grave.

'Honesty is a ruthless commodity. How honest can you be, Rosie, if I give you the choice of how you'd prefer to spend the evening—being gawped at and sniped at by my family, or discovering firsthand whether I'm as good a lover as I am a kisser?' Behind the glimmer of a mocking smile she detected an unexpected seriousness.

'Dinner suddenly seems a delightful proposition,' she said huskily. The fact that she needed to remind herself how much she hated him was very worrying.

'For a minute there…' He gave a smile that held mockery and possible disappointment. 'You might regret your decision in the near future,' he said, his eyes skimming over her outfit. He held his head on one side and considered her with an analytical expression.

Suddenly, taking her by surprise, he told her to lift her arms—and she complied. Three shirts were swiftly removed until she stood in the wine-coloured velvet body she wore beneath.

'You might be able to breathe more freely like that; also it seems a shame, even to prove a point, to hide your attributes. I'd say you're more generously endowed than your sister in that department. You look like a gypsy—very exotic.'

She pointed to her inelegantly shod foot and waved it, her heightened colour the only outward response to his observation. Inside all was chaos. 'Not very exotic.'

'You can carry it off; you have a certain…style,' he said confidently, making a graceful gesture with his hand. Was that a compliment? she wondered, casting him a startled look. 'You offered me a challenge, Rosie. When you know me a little better you'll understand that I can't resist a challenge.' His grey eyes glinted devilishly.

'Know you better?' she echoed drily. 'I can hardly wait,' she muttered as he stood to one side and saluted her with elegant mockery as she passed by.

AFTER THE FIRST FEW MOMENTS of breath-suspended fear she had actually enjoyed the sensation of travelling on the back of the gleaming black and chrome beast, but she had no intention of ever telling Morgan that. An appropriate steed for this particular Cinderella indeed!

'You can let go now,' he observed. 'This is called stationary.' He parked the motorcycle beside a stately Rolls-Royce, she noticed as she relinquished her hold around his waist and slid to the ground.

Stonily she handed him the crash helmet. 'Any more delightful surprises in store?' she enquired tartly, shaking her head and allowing her crushed hair to catch the breeze before it slid like a silent river of dark silk down her back.

He relieved her of the leather jacket he'd supplied. 'You enjoyed that,' he asserted confidently.

'Is there much insanity in your family?' she asked sweetly, following him up towards the brightly illuminated façade of the imposing house.

'My family tried to have my grandfather committed for a lesser sin than wearing jeans for a formal dinner,' he told her drily. 'So if a strait-jacket appears at some point don't be too alarmed.'

She gulped and slid into his tall shadow, not entirely sure how far he was stretching the truth. The liveried door attendant only blinked as they were ushered indoors and she was impressed by his self-restraint. She took a deep breath, feeling as if she was stepping into a tank of piranhas.

She turned from the sea of suddenly silent faces to cast a reproachful look at Morgan. The grey eyes were watching her with, she decided, malicious speculation; he was waiting for her to fall apart. With a bright smile her chin went up and, eyes sparkling, she calmly surveyed the aghast faces. She'd show him! If he could consider himself unrestrained by social conformity so could she.

'Fancy dress, Morgan?' His mother moved forward, detaching herself from the anonymous sea. She cast her son a tight, unamused look and offered Rosie an embrace that fell several centimetres short of her cheek.

'Rosie is very artistic.' By way of apology her father had joined them.

'No, I'm not,' she denied.

'Just perverse.' Morgan's contribution made her glance at him, her lips pursed and her eyes glittering with antagonism. 'A breath of fresh air, don't you think, Mother?' he drawled, a gleam of derision in his eyes.

'There is a time and place for fresh air. When I think of all the beautifully groomed women you could have...'

'This is my future wife, Mother, and I expect her to be treated accordingly.

'Mother is usually more subtle with her snubs, Rosie; you must really have her worried.' This mocking tone and not his original harsh castigation made the elegant elder woman flush. She gave them one last furious look before retreating to the hub of her family.

'Should I say thank you for that?' Rosie said, her eyebrows lifting in satirical enquiry. His next words proved that her scepticism had been well founded.

'From here on in you're on your own,' he said, projecting indifference with a casual lift of his shoulders. 'I'm too busy to be fighting your battles; you'll have to learn to look after yourself.'

She gave him a dazzling smile, her eyes as hard as his. 'What makes you think I'm not already more than capable?' she said calmly. Did he actually think he knew her on the basis of their brief and peculiar acquaintance?

She must never let the flashes of urbane, offbeat charm distract her from the fact that this was the real Morgan—ruthless, a shameless manipulator of people for his own purposes. He was ruining her life, blackmailing her in a totally shameless fashion and leaving her to literally sink or swim in a situation he had created.

She gave him a direct and scathing look of disdain and,

squaring her shoulders, sauntered away from him, her head held high.

Her hostess was not making her way any easier by introducing her, and most people seemed to be doing their well-bred best to ignore the fact that she was present. Rosie picked out a pleasant-looking man who looked approximately her own age and walked up to him. He looked reassuringly normal after Morgan's exclusive company and with a smile she introduced herself.

Their conversation gradually drew in a few of the younger guests nearest to them, and after a stilted beginning they all warmed to Rosie's easy, unselfconscious manner, and her dry humour had them laughing before long.

For no apparent reason, as she spoke to the personable young man, her eyes, as if pre-programmed, sought out Morgan. Meeting his intense, brooding stare, she found herself unable to look away. How had she known he was watching her? What internal alarm had alerted her? It wasn't just his attire that set him apart; he was easily the most striking man in a room of very attractive people. The Urquarts, it seemed, were blessed not only with money but also with more than their fair share of good looks.

She only half heard a laughing remark her companion made; she was still troubled by the look in the heavy-lidded eyes which had hit her with an impact that was almost physical. On the periphery of her vision she saw the familiar figure of Morgan's youthful admirer and she sighed with relief as dinner was announced. Ellie had been stalking her with a single-minded expression on her face that Rosie wasn't in the mood to deal with at that moment.

Her relief was short-lived; she had been seated between a woman who introduced herself as Ellie's mother and an elderly gentleman who was Morgan's uncle. The hostility that seeped from the pair was enough to ruin the flavour of the delicate and aromatic cucumber soup which was served.

Morgan had been placed as far from her as possible and

Ellie was beside him. She was intent on giving him her unswerving attention, Rosie saw. Did he enjoy it? she wondered. Or was that boredom she detected in his face? No; he intercepted her stare and then smiled in a charming, almost protective manner at something the girl said.

Perhaps they thought to separate me from any source of support, she thought ruefully. How wrong they were! Whilst she was deep in contemplation of this situation she had somehow got herself into, her elbow collided with the young girl removing the soup tureen and some of the contents splashed over her skirts.

The girl was very young and, judging from the accent revealed by her zealous apologies, French. Anxious to reassure her that it was her own fault entirely, Rosie smiled cheerfully, dismissing any damage and slipping unconsciously into the girl's native tongue as she did so. The incident neatly dealt with, she looked up to find herself the cynosure of all eyes.

Ellie's voice drifted clearly down the silent table, which was groaning beneath the weight of silver and crystal. 'Did she learn that French from a lover, do you think?'

Rosie's smile was casual. 'In a manner of speaking,' she agreed. 'He was my mother's. I speak Italian, German and can get by in Spanish,' she added, and her sphinx-like smile invited speculation. A giggle emanated from somewhere to her right but she simply applied herself to her food once more. Actually her school had been a very cosmopolitan establishment, and, though her mastery of several tongues had been polished during her travels, the foundations had been laid in a more conventional fashion.

'And how do you find English men after such variety?' her future mother-in-law enquired acidly.

'I'd have to sample an average cross-section before I could commit myself on that one,' she replied gravely. She was almost enjoying herself by this point. If they wanted moral laxity to turn their collective noses up at, she was more than willing to oblige.

'I believe your sister has.' This sally was greeted with a general titter, though some of the guests looked more uneasy than amused by the open malice.

The smile that curved Rosie's lips was placid but her sparkling eyes were a truer reflection of her feelings. Hearing her twin so scornfully spoken of filled her with a deep loathing of these smug, patronising people. 'Mother, dear, I'm more than happy to be the target of your ill-mannered malice but my sister is not here to defend her character.' The silence was awesome as her clear, rather deep voice resonated around the room. 'If you feel unable to comply, let me know and I'll leave.'

A reassessment was taking place behind the cool grey gaze of her hostess and Rosie, her knees shaking with reaction beneath the damask table covering, refused to lower her gaze first. When the elder woman looked away it was to her son, but no help was forthcoming there; he was at his most enigmatic and Rosie was aware without looking that it was her his eyes were fixed on.

'That seems a reasonable request.' The reply was a signal for the company to act as if the incident had never occurred. Well-bred amnesia, Rosie thought wryly.

After dinner, several of the younger members of the family began to dance to softly played music, not loud enough to offend the less energetically inclined.

'Delightful couple they make, Ellie and Morgan, but then they would,' commented Morgan's mother.

Rosie watched the girl pull Morgan to his feet and into the circle of dancing figures. 'Would they?' she said. Morgan's resistance had been minimal, she decided critically, watching him begin to move in time to the music. He bent his head to listen to something the girl said—protective and avuncular, or something less innocent...? She felt a sudden and alarming spasm of outrage, which would have been natural if their engagement had been of the normal variety; but, under the circumstances, it filled her with alarm.

'She's the living image of Rachel, but then that's not so surprising considering they were first cousins. They were the perfect couple—it's so tragic. I feel that Morgan sees Rachel every time he looks at Ellie.'

'That must be painful for him,' Rosie observed carefully, unwilling to reveal how little she knew of Morgan's marriage.

'She will have Morgan despite you.'

The hissed words made Rosie spin around. It occurred to her that Morgan's mother was just a trifle unbalanced; she was glaring at her with such a degree of malevolence that she took a step backwards.

'I believe Morgan will have something to say about that.' Did this woman really believe he was a man to be led by the nose? Morgan was a man who lived by his own rules; that was what made him so dangerous an adversary—as she'd learnt to her cost.

'You stole him from your own sister; we know what sort of woman we're dealing with.'

So that was the popular theory for the sudden substitution, was it? She was the general all-round bitch, out to catch the golden son. If she hadn't felt close to tears of pure frustration Rosie would have laughed out loud at the idea. She gave a faint smile, rather embarrassed by the other woman's unrestrained animosity; the desperation was somehow pitiful and sad.

'If you'll excuse me...'

Outside the open French doors there was a formal garden; neat box hedges led onto an ornamental garden in the Italian fashion, with a large, ornate pool as its centre and a fountain cascading into the shallow water. Sitting on the edge and drawing her knees up to her chin, she closed her eyes and listened to the soothing sound of the water.

She found herself puzzling over Morgan's marriage. Morgan in love... It was hard to believe. He was a passionately, intensely sensual man, but tender emotions? Was the similarity of the youthful Ellie's looks to his dead wife's the real reason he had looked elsewhere for a bride? Did he secretly hanker after her? The idea made her feel strangely dissatisfied.

She made a sound of anger and straightened up; Morgan Urquart was taking over her thoughts and that would never do. She peeled off the uncomfortable boots and stretched her hot feet, then, on an impulse, swung her feet into the water. It was blissfully cool and within a couple of minutes one thing had led to another and she was calf-deep in water, wading through the shallows, her skirts looped and tucked, peasant-fashion, in a bundle above her knees.

'Are you enjoying yourself?'

Rosie didn't look up; that tingling sensation between her shoulderblades had warned her of his presence just a fraction of a second before he'd spoken. 'It's a gift I have that in the midst of gloom and despondency I can take pleasure in the small things.' Her voice was a husky, sarcastic drawl.

'And are you despondent?'

'Ever the optimist, I'm hoping you'll come to your senses, or discover a hitherto untapped source of decency. What you're planning to do is...inhuman.' Her voice trembled with the pent-up emotion that she'd held in check all day. It had all seemed unreal, rather like walking through some particularly bizarre dream, but the painful reality of her situation hit her full force now and she was shaking with rejection.

'Optimism must be leavened with common sense, Rosie,' he said slowly, unapologetically, his eyes going from her stormy face to her bare legs dripping with water.

'It's certainly not sensible to consider the possibility that you're human,' she agreed wrathfully. 'I think you're pleased I arrived here like some freak, because you knew it would annoy your family.'

'The choice of outfit was your idea, sweetheart, but now you come to mention it,' he drawled, 'the situation has held a certain entertainment value.'

'They're all disgusting, pretentious snobs,' she burst out, her voice wobbling as she recalled the evening's nightmarish sequence of events. Her humiliation was just a mild diversion for him, she thought, loathing giving a new depth to her amber eyes. He was destroying her life yet he could be flippant.

'True, but you handled them rather better than I anticipated,' he admitted, placing one leather-covered foot on the wall. The flexing of his leg bunched the powerful muscles in his thigh and Rosie ripped her eyes from the spectacle, inwardly appalled at the irrational fascination that was no respecter of her wishes. 'Beautiful and brazen about sums up my mother's opinion of you. She admires people who stand up to her; not many do.'

'I've no wish to match my wits or my tongue with your mother's. I'm not some pet heretic, Morgan. What would she say if I told her why I'm actually marrying you?'

'Is that a threat?' He gave a mocking laugh. 'Can't you do any better than that? If you're looking to my family to rescue you, Rosie, you're doomed to disappointment.'

Rosie waded to the edge of the pool and impetuously caught his arm; the hard sinew and muscle beneath her fingers made her stomach muscles clench but didn't distract her from her purpose. 'If I could find someone willing to substitute, you could marry and keep your precious company.'

'You sound desperate.'

She searched his stony face and gave a sigh of frustration. 'That surprises you?' she said, tight-lipped. 'I am desperate *not* to marry a man I could only ever despise. I have a life, work; you haven't given a second thought to what you're robbing me of. Friends—'

'Lovers.' He interrupted her impassioned flow with biting contempt. 'You and your sister should have thought about that before you tried to cheat me. Irresponsibility isn't always made to pay the price, but this time it is. You're two of a kind—irresponsible social butterflies.' He sounded so cold, so implacable that hate tightened to a knot in her throat.

Hands akimbo on her hips, she didn't notice her skirts slither down into the water. 'You're the most selfish man I've ever met.' She shook her head and sent her hair flying around her shoulders. 'If you expect me to act like some besotted little idiot forget it. You may be able to blackmail me to the altar but I'll make your life as uncomfortable as I know how,' she promised.

'My sweet Rosie,' he observed, apparently amused by her threats, 'the majority of people will assume that you married me for my money anyway. If I thought there was any danger of you behaving like a lovesick teenager I'd terminate this arrangement immediately. And don't get ideas,' he advised as a hopeful expression swept over her face. 'I shall know any sudden changes of attitude for what they are.'

'Don't worry; my acting abilities fall short of that sort of role-playing. Besides, the idea makes me feel queasy.' She dug her foot into the water and kicked out, sending a shower of water over him. It was childish but at least it relieved some of her frustration. She decided to repeat the performance with even more vigour. This time her formerly immobile target shot out a hand, and it fastened around her slippery, wet ankle as firmly as any chain.

Rosie let out a squeal of protest and, arms clutching at empty air, fought to maintain her balance. Miraculously she did. 'Let me go,' she spluttered, balancing precariously on one leg.

'You have beautiful legs,' he observed, and despite her uncomfortable posture she froze, something in his voice—a rasping sensuality that licked the edges of his words—turning her defiant anger into uncertain fear. 'Delicate, elegant bones.'

Sweet mercy, she realised, she was responding to the husky intonation and the movement of his fingers over her cool, wet skin. One hand moved slowly down the curve of her calf and the other traced the arch of her finely boned, slim foot. Hand over hand he pulled her slowly towards him, forcing her to shuffle her free foot along the marble-bottomed pool.

'A graceful, sleek little cat,' he murmured. 'Do you purr, little cat, or scratch?'

'Let—me—go, Morgan…' Husky appeal filled her staccato, disjointed words. Looking into his gleaming eyes caused a sensation that was similar to that which she'd experienced in nightmares—a sense of falling into soft black darkness, of a total loss of control.

He stopped when her thigh rested against his hip. She was close enough to feel the throbbing hardness through the layers of her clothing. His desire should have repelled her—it had to be classed as impersonal. He didn't know her, he disliked her; cared nothing for her, just lust—common-or-garden lust—but there was nothing common about the sudden inferno that blazed inside her.

She was drawing in air as though her lungs had stopped working automatically. Impersonal sex was not something she had ever been tempted by; she was no thrill-seeker and had always considered sex without a deeper commitment sordid. The fact that her whole body was suffused with an explosive hunger was hateful to her…and oh, so attractive.

'If you think I'm going to pander to your inflated ego…' she said breathlessly. He slid one hand from her thigh to the curve of her behind and, with a movement that demonstrated a degree of strength that was stunning, swung her other foot off the floor until he supported her weight completely, her legs straddling his narrow hips and her body thrust against his.

Having succumbed to the savage impulse which her defiant beauty had elicited, Morgan met the golden-glazed haze in the eyes of the woman he held with animosity. He felt, perversely, that she had driven him to this display of brute strength, and despite the compulsive ache in his loins and the elemental hunger that would not be subdued by anything but her total surrender he had every intention of releasing her.

But at that moment a soft cry emerged from her lips and her head fell back, her body arched like a bow, even as her legs wrapped themselves around his waist, and his intention crumbled away to dust at that same moment.

Still supporting her, he sank to his knees, and, relieved of the burden of her weight, his hands slid up her spine to cradle her skull. The kiss didn't begin and build up; there was no subtlety, just a raw, explosive hunger which matched the energy that had built up inside him, demanding expression.

'So incredibly sensual, so sensitive.' The throaty words were murmured against her throat as his hands moved restlessly over her trembling body. 'The scent of your skin when it grows hot…' She heard the sound of him swallowing as if the action almost hurt him. 'I make you grow hot, Rosie.'

The words were drawing her further into the constricting inertia that held her in this warm, throbbing, sensual thrall. Her body had never been more achingly alive or sensitive, but the distinction between what this man was feeling and she was experiencing was slipping away, replaced by a need to merge…

'She's more dangerous than the sister…' The voice faded as footsteps moved away, and then it came again… 'He only wants the company; once he has that she'll be history.

You heard her flaunting her past... Morgan is far too fastidious to put up with that sort of behaviour for long.' The confident, distinctive twang of her future mother-in-law's voice carried distinctly on the soft evening breeze.

Rosie had already retreated physically and mentally from the scene she was a major player in. The words had had the authority of an oracle and she knew them to be more or less true. The humiliation of being such a willing...eager participant in such a... She gave a distressed groan and pulled away from him. Twisting sinuously, she rose to her feet with almost feline grace.

'Groping in the undergrowth smacks of the juvenile—or the desperate. You disappoint me; I expected something more...sophisticated.'

She was quite startled that out of the air she had managed to clutch and capture such sang-froid. Her heart was thudding hard enough for him to hear. Like a wounded animal she felt the need to escape and examine her wounds. Humiliation was strong enough to taste in her dry mouth...but the taste of him was stronger. He would gloat at her weakness, she was sure. Defiantly she met his glittering stare and she ached for him even as she hated him...madness!

The silence was disturbed only by the sound of their swift, laboured breathing. 'How fastidious of you, my dear,' he said slowly, watching her from beneath his heavy eyelids as he rose to his feet in one fluid motion. 'You lose control very easily; are you always so indiscriminate, or is this special?'

Special...? She was in a state of emotional turmoil and he was the cause. She let her anger bubble to the surface. 'I'd say it was you losing control,' she accused hotly. 'Mauling me around like a piece of meat!'

'And there's you hating every second.' He made a sound of complete disgust. '*I* can admit I find you exhilarating...in a physical sense. And in answer to your earlier comment I see nothing wrong in making love in any situation if it feels right. I've never been accused of lack of imagination.'

She blushed scarlet and tugged fretfully at the damp skirts that clung to her legs. 'It's not a question of where; it's more with whom.'

'So you keep saying, with boring frequency.' The grey eyes narrowed cynically. 'Methinks it's a case of the lady protesting a hell of a lot more than she should.'

'If it pleases you to think so…' She gave a bored shrug. She was still trying to come to terms with the treacherous way her own body had been hexed by this man's awesome masculinity. He had enough self-esteem to furnish a room full of megalomaniacs without her adding to it. She smiled, her teeth bared. 'You're the most selfish individual I've ever encountered.' She thought suddenly of her beautiful, aggravating mother and gave a wry smile. 'And I've seen some of those.'

Eyes still on her turbulent face, he bent forward and caught her discarded boots by the laces and threw them into the water.

'You are getting nothing more than you asked for.' The last glitter of passion had died from his eyes and they were hard and relentless. 'The Osborne girls should have thought twice before playing one of their little games with me. I stand to lose the company; everything my grandfather worked hard to achieve could go down the pan along with several hundred jobs. When you two were scheming I don't suppose for one minute you paused to take that into consideration?'

He eyed her with cold disdain and Rosie realised there was going to be no last-second reprieve for her…he meant to go through with it.

'You threw my boots into the water.' It was a problem that was easier to address than his ruthless logic.

'They were ugly.'

'Do the ends always justify the means?' Those husky words escaped at the same time as a solitary tear. They both knew she wasn't referring to her footwear any longer.

'Is that meant to prick my conscience?' he asked angrily, touching the wet track on her cheek with one finger and smiling thinly when she flinched. 'I can't physically force you to make the necessary responses tomorrow.'

'You're blackmailing—'

'Such melodrama,' he cut in scornfully. 'I'm using the tools I have; if one of them is your predilection for sisterly sacrifice…' The broad shoulders lifted.

She took a deep sigh and eyed him with abhorrence. 'I'm leaving now. Will you make my apologies to your charming mother?' Only the thought of her sister and Bill made her suppress her desire to walk away from him for ever.

'The gravel will cut your feet; I'll carry you.'

'I'd sooner walk on broken glass,' she informed him with deep sincerity.

'I'll send Donald out to the car; my driver will take you home. But don't try to run away, Rosie, because if you do there won't be a place secure enough to hide you from me.'

CHAPTER FIVE

ROSIE REFUSED TO BE REDUCED to the role of tragic martyr; glaring at her reflection in the hall mirror, she settled for bleak irritability. Her father was making the expected fulsome comments about beautiful brides but she couldn't actually concentrate on the words.

She did look chastely stunning in the acres of silk. The square-necked bodice encrusted with tiny seed-pearls seemed to have been inspired by the Elizabethan era, and the skirt, narrow in the front and sweeping out behind in an extravagant train, emphasised the narrowness of her waist and the dip and curve of her hips and thighs. The fine fabric, which rustled seductively as she walked, left her cold. She could only marvel at her sister's wanton extravagance, considering she had never intended it to be worn.

The limousine journey seemed to last an eternity. Beneath her veil her face felt stiff.

Some half an hour later, as she slowly repeated the required responses, a fury built up inside her. When the moment came and the symbol of her new bondage was slipped on her finger she finally looked at the man beside her. She noted the tightness around his sensual mouth and her reflection in the shuttered eyes; he was enduring a necessary evil, she reminded herself. One day she'd hurt him as much as he was her… She hung onto the savage notion like a talisman.

'ARE YOU PACKED?' He hadn't knocked and in a sharp, waspish tone she pointed this out. The reception at his mother's home had been an ordeal which had left her nervous system shattered. A packed marquee, horribly cheerful music, people she didn't know and the continuous flashes of light as cameras clicked away.

'How delightful—the coy bride.'

She swung around on the stool and tugged the light robe that was draped around her shoulders over the pale peach teddy she wore, fastening it tightly. His disturbing eyes had been tracing the curves of her body. 'The replacement bride,' she corrected. 'A fact which appears to have caused no end of speculation. Half the people here seem to think Elizabeth is absent because she's heartbroken about having the catch of the century cruelly snatched by her own sister.'

'We'll make every gossip column, but not the front page. Don't overestimate your importance, darling.'

'How comforting,' she snapped. 'And don't call me darling.' She grabbed a brush and sank it into her hair, tugging viciously, causing static to dance over her silky head.

'Try to look on it as lending a little colour to people's rather mundane lives.'

'I happen to like mundane.' She twisted round on the stool and glared at his reflection in the mirror. He loosened his tie, not in the least disconcerted by her scrutiny.

'Are you packed?' he repeated.

'Packed...what do you mean packed?'

'Suitable clothes for a honeymoon.'

'You have to be joking?' she breathed, giving an incredulous laugh. 'Isn't all this quite enough hypocrisy to be going on with?'

'Your sister was quite insistent; everything has been arranged on a lavish and ostentatious scale. But I imagine she thought I'd be languishing on a beach all alone. Was she delighted to hear that I shall have company after all?'

'I haven't told her,' Rosie admitted.

A dark brow quirked. 'How noble,' he sneered.

'There wasn't much she could do, was there? I saw no point in blighting *her* marriage. You can't honestly expect me to go on a honeymoon.' Her mouth twisted with scorn.

'I expect just that.'

'You can save that lord-of-all-I-survey tone for those who are impressed,' she said airily. Who did he think he was?

'Right now I am lord of all—or rather whom—I survey,' he pointed out with maddening calm. 'I expect you to fill your obligations to the letter, Rosie. Your sister chose white...you wore it—an inspired choice,' he observed drily. 'She chose to languish in the sun, and she agreed to bear my child.'

The last reminder made her grow paler; her skin glowed like marble and Morgan found himself wondering whether it would feel as cold and unearthly to the touch. He watched her hands move shakily from the waist of her robe to the collar, which she clutched with trembling fingers.

'I hate sunbathing.'

'I'm sure we'll think of something to do...people generally do on honeymoons.'

'I think you're coarse and disgusting.' His smile was unashamedly wicked and quite unique. I need my hormones regulated, she decided despairingly as her skin began to generate a sudden blast of heat.

'I didn't think you'd have packed so I sent one of my people to do it for you.'

She made a choking noise in her throat. 'How dare you?'

'Have you been to the Bahamas before?' he enquired with mild interest. 'We have family connections that go way back.'

'Then I'm bound to hate it.' Her even white teeth ground achingly together.

'That's what I like—an open mind.'

A maid appeared just as she launched the first missile

that came to hand at Morgan. The brush hit the maid on her ear.

Morgan's laughing apology turned the girl's startled look to one of gaping adoration in three seconds. Rosie shot him a murderous look when he stated that she liked to play rough; he hadn't seen anything yet, she told herself stoutly, unwilling to admit that he had thwarted her at every turn so far.

'I can manage on my own, thank you,' she said when the girl's errand was explained.

'Tell my mother I'm helping,' Morgan called after the blushing young woman. 'Seems you tore this trying to escape in a hurry,' he observed as he retrieved the heavily embroidered silk gown from the crumpled heap on the floor.

'I did have an impulse to tear it into shreds,' she admitted. 'But I decided to give it to the nearest charity shop.'

'I think you'll find there is limited call for designer bridal gowns.'

'*I* have little use for a designer wedding gown.'

'Is that a promise of eternal commitment? How sweet.' She met his mocking eyes in the mirror and compressed her lips into a thin line. I won't rise to the bait...I won't, she told herself.

'I was thinking along the lines of auction; they do that kind of thing to raise money. It gives the rich and idle a chance to feel benevolent.' Would she always come off worst when matching his cutting quips? she wondered wearily.

'Is Mrs Urquart going to get deeply involved in charitable acts?'

'No matter what the paper says I'll never be Mrs Urquart.' She pressed her hand to her breast and her eyes blazed. 'Not in here,' she choked.

'You must be anatomically unique if you have your name emblazoned somewhere in the thoracic cavity. Or is this your soul you're getting so passionate about? If so, don't be concerned. I've no interest in that...'

The pain was sudden and dull-edged, but it made her bite her lip. This verbal confirmation of what she already knew shouldn't have the power to hurt this badly...so why...? She banished the persistent question and elevated her chin by several degrees.

'The market value isn't high enough, I expect.'

'Value is relative. But you're right—no woman is worth all the angst involved in heart-to-heart encounters.'

His cynicism was so strong, she found it repugnant. 'Not even Rachel?'

The languid mockery was banished in the space of a single breath. 'What do you know about Rachel?'

He took a threatening step towards her but didn't touch her. His face was hard and set, and his eyes held accusing distaste; her words had put him on the defensive; why? That was the puzzling thing. Was she not allowed to utter so much as the name of his sainted wife? she wondered.

'I know she was your wife.'

He scrutinised her with brutal objectivity for a second and then seemed to relax slightly. 'I prefer *you* not to discuss her. Is that clear?' The silky thread of warning was distinct in every syllable.

'I agree she must have been a saint to have married you.' Her smile was deliberately taunting; the iron man had a vulnerability and she was going to find out one way or another what precisely it was.

Even if it hurts? she asked herself. But why should it hurt? Rachel Urquart is nothing to me but she is the only person he appears to have cared about more than himself. Was that the case when she was alive? she wondered.

'How did she die?' she asked him.

The fingers that bit into her collar-bone felt as if they'd crush her. 'You are here to share a very limited part of my life, Rosie. Don't stray into areas that are none of your concern. Or you might regret your ghoulish curiosity.' He lifted his hands and his sensual mouth curled contemptuously at one corner. 'We have a plane to catch.'

She heard the door slam and closed her eyes, allowing her body to droop. At least he'd lost interest in helping her to dress; that at least should have pleased her… The question was, did it? Horror-struck at the answer that leapt into her mind, she gave a faint moan.

THE FLIGHT TO NASSAU was uneventful and smooth. She pretended to sleep and apparently Morgan did not feel inclined to expose the illusion—perhaps he had no more wish to converse with her than she did with him. The thought was depressing and she cursed her perversity. Loathing and deep physical attraction were difficult feelings to marry. Marriage…Mrs Urquart… She forgot her comatose stance and opened her eyes to slide the band of gold across her finger as far as the knuckle.

'Leave it on or people will think we're heading for an illicit assignation.'

'I thought you were above caring what people think.'

'I'm trying to establish us as a married couple.'

'Create an illusion,' she accused bitterly. 'Why bother?'

'I'd like a stable environment in which to raise my child.'

'A bit premature, aren't we?' She used her not inconsiderable will-power to banish the vivid images of children with grey eyes and pale golden hair which had suddenly flashed into her mind; the emotion they stirred within her was powerful. She was never going to play happy families with this man. There had to be some way to escape.

'I've never been accused of bad timing.'

Superficially innocent, the words were lent an entirely different meaning by the heavy-lidded stare accompanying them. She felt hot colour wash over her skin, and the process was accelerated when he laughed—a low, incredibly sexy sound. A flurry of activity indicated that it was time for them to disembark; her legs felt almost tremulous and she avoided his guiding hand as though her life depended on it. She thought maybe her pride depended on it—less dramatic but just as important.

Even though it was late the heat and brightness outside assaulted her senses. It was like walking out of a sepia print into brilliant Technicolor: disorientating. The light linen suit she had worn in London had seemed suitable summer garb, but here Rosie felt over-dressed.

'Is the hotel far?' she asked, feeling like a well-fried lettuce leaf within two minutes.

'Hotel? We're not staying in a hotel.'

'What are we doing, then—camping on the beach?' she snapped.

'We're staying on Sarisa.'

'Your boat?'

'My island.'

She gaped at him, shading her eyes against the glare of the sun. Why didn't the heat affect him? she wondered resentfully. His cream trousers were uncreased and his open-necked shirt looked enviably cool. 'You own an island?'

'A very small one,' he confirmed blandly.

HE WOULD BE A PILOT, of course, she decided as an hour later the Piper Navajo took off from the private airstrip. His list of accomplishments would probably fill a book.

As necks and jaws went his were just about perfect; seated slightly to the rear of him, she had an excellent view of the back of his neck and jawline; she could see all the details of his firm square jaw and cleft chin.

'If you can tear your eyes away the view is worth a second glance. I get distinctly nervous when you eye up my jugular like that.'

It was mortifying to be caught staring like some silly schoolgirl. 'How far is it to Sa...?'

'Sarisa. South of Eluthera and east of Exuma.'

'Which tells me absolutely nothing.'

'We'll be there soon, Rosie; just chill out, angel. People out here don't rush—not in the outer islands.'

'I think I can promise to be chilly,' she announced primly, hoping that this was true. The view—blue, heavenly—was close enough to many people's ideas of heaven but right at that moment her appreciation was limited. 'There seem to be a lot of islands,' she observed in a desultory fashion at one point. The closer to their destination they came, the greater her nerves stretched.

He gave her a sideways glance. 'Seven hundred in all, give or take.'

'How did you come to have one?'

'A great-uncle left it to me; he had no kids of his own and didn't get on too well with most of the family. He was my grandfather's brother. Grandfather inherited the family estate and all the trappings, but Uncle Charlie made his own fortune and brought Sarisa with his ill-gotten gains. You could say Sarisa is the consequence of a misspent youth.'

'Genetics have a lot to answer for,' she remarked, resting her chin on her cupped hands.

'He came out here in the twenties and, to cut a long and occasionally lurid story short, made his fortune running liquor to the States during Prohibition.'

'Wasn't that illegal?'

'Only in the States,' he said with a piratical grin, all charm and eighteen-carat danger. She could only too easily see him as a modern-day pirate, too, as his charismatic charm reached out and touched her. 'The situation was by no means unique, Rosie; it was the way many fortunes were made.'

Although she was a hardened traveller, the landing made her catch her breath. As the plane swept in over a wide expanse of sand it felt as though they were gliding in to meet the ocean. 'Welcome to paradise,' Morgan said as they touched down.

'Complete with the serpent.'

A four-wheel drive was waiting for them and mercifully it was air-conditioned. The light was fading fast now and her impressions of her surroundings were vague.

Morgan sat in the front with the lanky man who had met them and they conversed in low voices, excluding her completely. She was jolted along an uneven dirt track until they reached their destination.

She slid to the ground and stared, transfixed. 'I don't believe this.' Sugar-pink, the gracious colonial mansion rose out of the subtropical scrub.

'It was transported out here stone by stone from Virginia by the loyalist family who originally settled the island,' Morgan explained, watching her reaction. 'They came complete with slaves to reconstruct their cotton plantation.'

Enchanted by the entirely unexpected vision, Rosie smiled. 'Did they succeed?'

'Alas, no; Sarisa is basically a lump of limestone, shallow soil, so the venture ultimately failed. When Charlie bought the place it was just a shell; he lavished a lot of care on it in order to make it habitable. Are you a closet romantic, Rosie?' he asked, watching the emotions flit across her face. 'They were doomed to failure, you know; people unable to adapt usually are. Trying to re-create the past is always a mistake.'

'All that effort,' she observed sadly, still overawed by the task those long-ago folk had attempted. 'It seems a pity.' She lengthened her stride to keep up with him.

'Don't feel too sorry, Rosie; if local legend is true the family made a new fortune gun-running for the Confederacy during the Civil War. With it they bade a relieved farewell to Sarisa.'

'The place appears to attract pirates in one form or another,' she observed drily.

Morgan gave her an enigmatic grin and pushed open the door. Rosie stepped past him on the veranda and indoors. With dark polished wood and white walls, the hallway was galleried and the ground-floor doors opening off it all stood open; it was light, cool and fragrant. Splashes of colour adorned the walls, and the quality of the art made her eyes widen. Had these been accumulated by Morgan, or his uncle? she wondered, impressed by the assembled talent.

A short, plump woman emerged and threw her arms around Morgan's waist. 'About time you brought your woman.'

The accent was unusual and attractive, and Rosie met the frankly curious stare unoffended; it held no animosity and the grin that broke out was as dazzling as the sun. The hug she received was rib-crushing and she met Morgan's amused look over the woman's shoulder and fought the impulse to smile back. Smile…? She must be mad; she had been forced, coerced and blackmailed here and she had nothing to smile about. Especially when she thought about her wedding night.

She thought about it now as she was released and the colour in her face faded dramatically.

'Mr Morgan, this child looks tired enough to drop. What have you been doing with her?'

'It's been a long flight…a long day,' Rosie said, with a faintly apologetic smile. This concern was extremely unusual; her welfare was not high on anyone's list of priorities. Tears of emotion began to well in her eyes and she blinked. Self-pity, Rosie, will get you nowhere, girl; stay tough, she admonished herself sternly. Kind words somehow went places she had sealed off from harsher attacks. Fortunately Morgan was never likely to discover this.

'This is Sally, Rosie; she looks after Sarisa.'

The seamed face still appeared concerned. 'Your man can take you on up to your room and I'll send on up some food. Mr Morgan, this girl needs rest so you keep your hands to yourself.' The deep, throaty chuckle bounced off the ceiling.

'There's a sentiment I can identify with,' Rosie breathed as she mounted the wide, sweeping staircase beside him.

'Was the wilting-flower act for Sally's benefit, then?' he asked. 'You seem to have rediscovered your claws rather swiftly.' His voice echoed his scepticism.

'I was just shocked by anyone actually being concerned for my welfare,' she shot back sarcastically. Stiff-backed, she walked into the room he indicated.

She took a deep breath; flowers of all descriptions were stuffed into an assortment of containers. The perfume was overpowering, as was the view from the doors that opened onto a wide balcony. The sun was starting to sink behind the horizon and the sea was touched by fingers of blood-red. She stayed still for a moment in silent appreciation.

Her eyes slid to the enormous canopied bed that dominated the room and her eyes rose of their own accord to the silent man beside her. A stark silence filled the room and she felt as if she was falling into the secretive depths of his extraordinary eyes.

His eyes touched the dark smudges beneath her eyes, and a flicker of... No, never concern, she decided; not from him, not for her.

'You look like hell.'

'Thank you, but that's generally a place. Home is where the heart is...hell is where you are, Morgan.' Her voice was tight, emotion-packed.

'Then you had better get used to it, sweetheart, because I intend to keep you close at hand.' His nostrils flared as he eyed her with indifferent animosity.

Then he was gone, and she headed for the bathroom, peeling off her travel-stained garments, and stepped beneath a warm, reviving shower. What an absurd situation to be in: fatally attracted to a man who was her husband. It shouldn't, in a sane world, have been the ultimate in humiliation, but under these unique circumstances it was. Every time she looked at him she was aware of a barrage of unfulfilled longings, and they overwhelmed and confused her.

If this ruthless manipulator realised the extent of her vulnerability and just how singular her reaction to him was he would use it for his own ends; she knew that. There was no softness, no gentleness despite the fact that he was open about his physical desire for her; as a person she was less than nothing to him. In forcing this marriage on her he had proved just how easily he was prepared to sacrifice her.

Wearing a thin cotton shift nightdress she had pulled from her case, she slid beneath the cool sheets, and by the time Sally arrived with a tray she had already been lulled into sleep by the distant sound of the waves breaking on the shore.

SHE WOKE DISORIENTATED and filled with a nebulous sense of dread. As she sat up her eyes encountered a steady grey regard that gave substance to her fears. How long had he watched her? She shivered; the situation seemed somehow symbolic of her new vulnerability. The room was filled with moonlight and it turned his dull-gold hair moon-silver; the light was like a faint nimbus around his head. His gaze was indecipherable through the thick, straight fringe of his dark lashes.

'What time is it?'

'One a.m.'

She cleared her dry throat. 'I fell asleep,' she said somewhat unnecessarily.

'Sally's left some cold stuff in the kitchen; I'll fetch it if you like.'

She felt the cool air and his eyes touch her flesh simultaneously.

She wore only the thin cotton shift, and in the moonlight it was almost transparent—the *almost* was the most arousing part of the picture, Morgan decided, slowly lifting his heavy-lidded gaze back to her face. A muscle leapt in his lean cheek. Her breasts were full and high, thrust against the fabric, and he saw the rosy peaks harden under his eyes.

'Just a drink; my throat's a little dry.' It was closing up as emotions rose to suffocate and overwhelm her. Had a man ever looked at her like that before? If so she had never been receptive to it, not to unadorned sensuality on a level that was almost primeval. She had no defence for the rioting sensations that throbbed inside her; mundane words were doing nothing to disguise the true situation.

'There's some fruit juice here.' He stretched forward and pulled a jug that lay on a side table towards himself; the ice played a faint, discordant melody as it hit the cut glass.

Rosie watched the sinews in his forearm tighten beneath his tanned skin as he lifted the jug. Her heart had slowed to a strong, steady rhythm; was it expectancy? she wondered. A soft sound escaped her lips and he looked up, enquiry in his face.

'I hope I haven't put Sally to too much trouble,' she said to cover the awkward moment.

'Sally is a creature of extremes; if she likes you nothing is too much trouble; if not...' The shrug was expressive.

'Does she live here?'

'She has a bungalow in the grounds so we are all alone.'

The rich texture of his voice made her pluck nervously at the neckline of her nightgown; no man had the right to sound so blatantly sexy. 'A big house for one woman. I hope she has help.' Her laugh was strained and unnaturally bright.

A finger pressed to her lips stilled the sound; his thumb exerted soft pressure, as if to test the cushiony invitation of the pink-tinted flesh, before falling away. 'Sally has plenty of help, and virtually a free hand here at Sarisa. She was much more than Uncle Charlie's housekeeper.'

He paused to allow the import of his words to sink in.

'If she'd allowed me I'd have signed the place over to her; she has much more right to it than me. But she wouldn't hear of it. She likes the situation as it is and I can only respect her wishes. The only thing she craves is children to cosset; perhaps that's why she's welcomed you with open arms.'

The allusion to the bottom line of their alliance made Rosie's skin prickle, and heat scorched her flesh. She had zealously been avoiding thinking along those lines, but now that he'd mentioned children the part of the equation that made them possible refused to be consigned to the back-burner.

She accepted the drink carefully, avoiding contact with his fingers, and swallowed deeply. 'I think we should lay a few ground rules,' she began briskly, but a shiver that curled insidiously up the length of her spine all but robbed her of speech.

'What did you have in mind?' he enquired with interest, and his smile, blindingly predatory, tinged with cynicism, deepened as she stared back dumbly. He removed the empty glass from her slack grasp. 'You want me, Rosie.'

The unvarnished statement made her suck in her breath; his confidence should have infuriated her but her body was aching; her co-ordination had deserted her as completely as her speech.

'Why the horror?' he asked harshly. 'Shouldn't we both be grateful for harmony, at least on a chemical level?' The rider sounded curiously bitter.

'Please...Morgan...please,' she said huskily; the tremors that had begun to shake her body were visible now.

'Why this persistent denial of the obvious?' he continued, ignoring her plea—in fact it appeared to have made him angry. 'I've wanted you since the first time I touched you,' he said throatily.

Survival, she wanted to say; she had to deny what she felt...she felt too much, and when he realised that, as he ultimately would, he'd be repelled, or, even worse, amused by the fact. He had no place in his life for love… Love! What was she thinking? She flung back the covers and swung her legs clear of the bed, filled with a sudden desire to escape from him and the direction of her thoughts.

A hand on her chest pushed her back onto the mattress. Shapely fingers splayed, the hand slid down to her ribcage, whilst the other one took his weight as he leaned over her. 'Where exactly are you running to?' The words emerged from compressed lips; she closed her eyes to shut out his face and his slitted eyes, filled with passion and nothing else, peculiarly blind. It was frightening and her closed, delicate eyelids couldn't wipe the image from her mind's eye. She could feel his breath on her skin and smell the musky male scent that came from his body.

'You can't force…' She could taste the blood on her lips where she'd bitten the tender flesh.

'Force!' The muttered expletive that followed made her wince. 'You'd feel happier if that were the case, wouldn't you?' he accused. 'It's the fact that it never would be that that really gets to you. You want to play the martyr to the hilt; next you'll be telling me you're the complete innocent. Looking at me with those big hurt eyes… Do you really think I'm going to fall for all that pathos? Your appetite is as healthy as mine.'

'Not for you…'

'Then you'll hate this,' he murmured throatily, and his hand slid inside her shift, up the smooth curve of her thigh, across her belly, and came to rest on one rounded breast. The mound of firm flesh quivered and swelled in his hand.

The swift, unerring journey made a nonsense of her protests. All her denials dissolved as a flood of intense, dizzying excitement overwhelmed her.

'Do you hate this?' He had dispensed with her inadequate garment in one bewildering motion and his eyes, glittering now, feasted themselves on her pale form, which was gleaming in the moonlight. The sight of her slim, supple curves glowing in the other-worldly light made his eyes grow almost savage. This was no statue, but flesh and blood, warm and receptive, waiting for him to mould it. He fought to keep the searing heat inside him under control; the effort made his chest swell and the muscles in his throat work hard.

'No, I don't.'

The words were faint and indistinct but he must have heard her; the triumphant curve of his sinfully sensual mouth told her that. She felt the touch of his lips on one sensitive breast, moving with inevitable certainty to the hardened nipple. Her body was convulsed by a burning sensation as his teeth and tongue worked a painful magic; it was an addictive sensation and she made a small, guttural noise of protest as he lifted his head. The shudder of voluptuous pleasure came as he gave a similar treatment to the hitherto neglected breast.

With devastating skill his fingers and mouth moved over her supine form. When he eventually claimed her mouth she was desperate to the point of tears to taste him.

'That's it, sweetheart,' he murmured huskily against her skin, encouraging her hands as they slid beneath his shirt, embracing the hard, sculpted curves of his torso with trembling eagerness.

Rosie felt as if she'd plunged headlong into a maelstrom of pure sensuality; she was driven by a primeval programming that overrode her normal restraint.

He kneeled and completed her task of removing his shirt; never once did his eyes leave her. The rest of his clothes followed—too slowly, too erotically; she felt as if her eyelids covered molten pools. He was truly glorious, every greyhound-lean line of him exuding unsubdued power. He took her breath away. The sight of male arousal did not reduce her to virginal modesty; she felt pure, uninhibited appreciation. He was incredibly beautiful. She wanted to touch him again.

'I'm glad.'

Had she actually said it? she wondered. But as she returned to her sensual exploration it didn't seem to matter; all that mattered was the feel of his flesh beneath her fingers, his hoarse sounds of pleasure as he urged her on, the dizzying and unexpected sense of feminine power. She felt unchained, released.

Her restraint had disappeared with his touch, with his quest to experience the tactile pleasure of her female form. She welcomed the intimacy of his new caress but was aware of a building frustration, a hunger to have more…

Her cry of amazement and sweet pain as he slid fiercely into the warm recesses of her body brought forth an answering cry from his throat…anger? Triumph? She was in no condition to analyse; she was simply going with the ebb and flow, the rhythm that filled her mind, her body. The swift, unexpected spasm that caught her in its coils was mind-blowing. Gasping and shaking, she subsided as he rolled away from her, his powerful frame still racked by shudders.

Lying on her back, she lifted her hand to her face and felt her cheeks; they were wet with tears which were still falling. Morgan was lying very still beside her and she could hear the sound of his breathing. Steeling herself, she turned her head and looked at him. Even now, in this sexually quiescent state, the sheer magnificence of him moved her deeply. He had one arm raised, thrown across his eyes. At this point she should have been able to burrow into him and let sleep claim her, to revel in her new-found sensuality. Deep sadness filled her as she realised that, passion spent, she no longer had the intimacy she craved for.

She had always imagined that she had a will-power of steel—either that or a very low sex drive. The truth of the matter was that she hadn't had any trouble resisting temptation because she had never actually had her restraint tested before.

The first time and I crumble, she thought. But could she regret that glorious oblivion in his arms? No—even if those arms had no time for her now. The experience had been precious, emotional and physical combined...love... What was love? She shot him another glance and this time his eyes were fixed on her.

CHAPTER SIX

THE CLASH OF THEIR EYES totally engrossed her; she forgot other details; the heap of tangled bedclothes on the floor, their naked skin exposed to the warm, slightly humid night air. She succumbed without a battle to the probing interrogation of his silver-grey gaze.

'How the hell have you managed to hold on to virgin status?' he demanded eventually, sitting upright. His face was still and controlled, the turbulence in his eyes standing out in violent contrast.

Reality intruded very successfully into the quiescent, languid state that had prevented her from thinking too much about where they would go from this point. She reached for the covers and found none available; rather than appear foolish, she tried to act as if she was at ease with her nude state. It wasn't easy; she was suffering an agony of self-consciousness. She hoped that the semi-light concealed some of her discomfiture.

'Good fortune rather than strategy,' she replied flippantly. Defences could be rebuilt, she decided, her jaw hardening.

'You mean you get more out of men by withholding what they want.' He gave a hard laugh. 'I've married a professional virgin!' he exclaimed, with enough derision to send a knife-blade slicing through her. 'Maybe I was wrong about your motivations in substituting for your sister,' he suggested broodingly. 'Maybe you've been holding out for a rich husband, and I happened along providentially, my sweet virgin bride,' he sneered.

'I can hardly claim that unique status now, can I? You should have troubled to check me out the way you did Elizabeth. How embarrassing it would be if my past should reappear to haunt you.'

My past is more likely to lull him to sleep, she thought wryly; but let him worry. Had her mother's wearisome stream of lovers made her inherently wary of surrendering herself on some trivial impulse? she wondered. Her inexperience had never been something that had worried her: someone would come along… At the back of her mind that naïve certainty had taken root. And someone had. She swallowed, her throat working furiously to overcome the rising constriction.

A frown furrowed Morgan's brow and she had the impression that he wasn't actually listening to her; Morgan was dealing with a problem and she was worrying about the answers he might come up with. The last thing he wanted was a wife in love with him; he had been brutally frank about that. If he suspected what she herself could no longer deny… She inwardly cringed at the thought. She had to be insane. Why this man, of all men?

'I can't believe a woman as sensual and sexually uninhibited as you are can have only just discovered sex.' His eyes ran over her recumbent form and her skin was suffused with a rosy glow.

'I've just been successfully seduced; I never claimed to be sexually unaware. I'm just deeply sorry that what I've been saving for someone special was wasted on you.'

He flinched visibly under the acid assault of her words and dull colour emerged through his even tan. 'No seduction was required, Rosie; you were eager enough. So if you've any idea of implying that I resorted to brute force…' he grated. 'Am I supposed to be overcome by remorse for sullying your innocence? The fact is, sweetheart, you enjoyed being sullied.'

With an impetuous movement she swung her legs over the side of the bed and picked up the antique patchwork counterpane. She wrapped it around herself sarong-style and stalked to the other side of the room, into the shadow; it was safer. 'How would I dare imply anything of the sort? After all, we're talking about the sort of morally incorruptible person who thinks nothing of blackmailing a person into marriage.'

'That's a separate issue entirely.'

She expelled a furious breath. 'How can you say that?' she said scornfully. 'Do you think I'd have been there in your bed if you hadn't used the most underhand tactics possible?' Overwrought tears overflowed, to be impatiently blotted with the back of her hand.

'If we'd met under different circumstances, who knows...?'

'I know,' she burst out. 'I despise everything about you, and even if I didn't I'd never get involved with an emotional cripple. You don't care about anything or anyone.' She flung the accusations at him as if they were solid objects, hoping one would find its target, but she doubted any would; he seemed immune.

He ran his long, sensitive fingers through his hair—elegant, shapely fingers; she gave a small, voluptuous shiver as she recalled their touch... 'Why didn't you tell me you were a virgin before we actually got married?'

'Are you about to tell me you have scruples?' Her laughter bordered on the hysterical. 'Besides, would you have believed me?' How did he have the gall to sound indignant? she asked herself.

The grey eyes half closed and his head tilted back as he eyed her clinically. 'Probably not,' he conceded, his lips twisting. 'But then considering the track record of your closest female relatives I can hardly be blamed for the obvious conclusions I drew. Hasn't it occurred to you that I didn't want to be your first sexual experience?' he said harshly. 'If you've been repressing your sexuality for this long I've no doubt you'd have fallen like a ripe peach for any man who happened along at the right moment. I have no illusions on that score.'

She ought to feel grateful for small mercies, she told herself. He hadn't even wanted what she had given him; he certainly wouldn't want any impetuous avowals of her love. Thank God she had managed to conceal that much at least!

'I'm overcome by your faith in my ability to discriminate,' she breathed wrathfully. 'I'm sure you'll be equally understanding when I want to try out my burgeoning skills…sample what life has to offer for the sexually active female.'

At this he rose to his feet, but he didn't follow her lead and wrap himself in bedlinen. He was unashamedly naked, imposingly tall, gracefully strong and gloriously pagan—enough to make her breath emerge as a sigh as an appreciative thrill ripped through her. 'If you want to know about sex I'll be your tutor,' he said in a tone that contained a silky thread of warning.

'I've only your words that you're the expert,' she retorted pertly. The quilt slipped, showing the upper curve of her breasts, but she didn't retrieve it. 'Besides, I know how precious your valuable time is.' From heartbreak to recklessness was an easy step, she discovered; just then she wanted to hurt him with a depth of passion that was vaguely shocking.

He covered the space between them in three paces and his fingers made painful points of pressure in the flesh of her wrists. He slid his hands into hers and, their fingers interlaced, held them up between them. 'You might get more than you bargained for with that sort of provocation,' he told her in a rasping, throaty voice that was incredibly erotic. 'But then perhaps that's what you intended.'

'Morgan...' Panic at what she had done made her twist in his grip. 'I don't want...' she denied tremulously.

'Oh, but you do. I think we've established that beyond any shadow of a doubt. We both want... I couldn't understand why a woman I had thought was beautiful had suddenly become painfully desirable.' She stopped struggling, fascination tightening in her throat. He was talking in such a compulsive way, and his eyes held a mesmerising, wild gleam. 'One left me cold, if appreciative, the other...'

He took a deep breath, causing his muscle-packed shoulders to heave. 'I'm more than willing to help you explore your sensuality, Rosie. I don't think you'll find it too much of a strain to confine your activities to the marriage bed.' His tongue dived deep into the moist, honeyed recesses of her mouth and he drank her in as though he was parched for her unique flavour.

She tried to remind herself that their bed was like every other part of their marriage—an empty sham, a cold-blooded exercise in manipulating circumstances to suit Morgan Urquart. But she lost the battle even before he placed her back on the bed and joined her.

'I want everything from you,' he breathed against her sweat-slick skin moments later. And the primitive desire to gratify that wish was with her until, at almost dawn, exhaustion finally claimed her.

THE FOLLOWING MORNING she awoke alone; she tried to feel pleased about the fact. What could have been worse than facing Morgan across the breakfast table, with all the memories of the night before fresh in their minds? In the light of day her lack of inhibitions was distinctly disturbing.

Dressed in light cotton shorts and a matching sleeveless top, she finally made her way downstairs. After trying several rooms she discovered the kitchen and Sally.

'Come along in, child, and let me fatten you up.'

Obediently Rosie sat herself at a long, scrubbed table. 'Your man was up real early and he says to let you sleep...' The husky chuckle brought twin flags of colour to Rosie's cheeks. 'Though why a man with a lovely new bride locks himself away in that office all the morning long puzzles me.' She clicked her tongue disapprovingly. 'You take your coffee along in and keep him company. I'm sure he don't mean you when he says, "No visitors."' She dropped her voice to a passable imitation of Morgan's bass tones.

'Actually I'm dying to see the island. I thought I'd explore.'

The sniff was remarkably articulate. 'As you like. Cover up and use plenty of cream,' she warned as Rosie excused herself.

The gardens surrounding the house merged almost imperceptibly into the natural, intensely green scrub. Beyond it lay the sugary white sand of an enormous bay. Removing her sandals and placing her bare feet on the sand, she felt as if hers were the first to mar the virginal perfection. The only sounds were the ocean, crystalline and shimmering, and an occasional sea bird's cry.

Lost in deep contemplation, she'd walked the mile of the bay's length before she stopped. This end of the bay was rockier, and the lush undergrowth crawled over the rocks to overhang the water. She flopped down on the sand and promptly fell asleep.

She was awoken by a hand roughly shaking her.

'Morgan, what the...?' she began indignantly.

His face was dark with anger. 'Asleep in the sun at midday, without even a hat. Have you never heard of heatstroke? Sally was concerned; she dragged me out to search for you. She sent this.' He crammed a straw hat with a wide brim onto her head. 'I told her you had more sense but she obviously recognises a lunatic when she sees one.'

'I'm sorry you were disturbed,' she said haughtily, bringing her knees up to her chin and resting her head on them. 'Don't let me keep you.'

The shadow along his jawline suggested he hadn't shaved, and his hair wasn't as sleek and well ordered as usual. Cut-off blue denims and no shirt completed his apparel and her eyes moved covetously over the oiled, smooth flesh of his chest and belly before sliding to the long, powerful length of his legs. The casual beachcomber garb didn't disguise the strength and danger of the man.

'It's lunchtime and you've had enough sun for one morning,' he said, still critical, but less scathing now.

'You're not my keeper,' she returned truculently. She averted her eyes with incredible difficulty and a sensation akin to suffocation rose, warm and clogging, to occlude her throat. Just looking at him could make her legs grow numb; the rush of blood bathed her hot skin in sudden heat.

He grabbed her hand and pulled her to her feet. 'You need one, it would seem.'

'I thought you were going to leave me to my own devices,' she reminded him, rubbing the soft sand from the seat of her shorts as he released her hand. Nothing in his manner suggested they were anything more than acquaintances—passionate acquaintances. He couldn't have made it plainer how little the previous night meant to him. An intimacy that had been beyond anything her imagination had ever conjured up had now been replaced by dispassionate irritation.

'The consequences of that would be having a sick female on my hands.'

She made a disparaging noise, thinking he was making a fuss about nothing—something she told him forcibly.

'You should never underestimate the power of the sun. People do every year, and spend their holidays being treated for dehydration and fed by intravenous drip,' he said with an air of exasperation at her blatant irresponsibility.

'As Sally has made such an effort, I think you should at least put in an appearance.'

'I didn't intend to fall asleep; I was tired.' Falling reluctantly in step with him, she made an attempt to justify herself. The look he shot her made her wish she'd phrased that differently.

'I'm not surprised,' he observed drily, and she dropped her tawny eyes, flushing wildly. 'Don't you think embarrassment is a little misplaced between us?'

'Don't you need sleep?' she asked, diplomatically not challenging this dry statement. Last night had happened; it hadn't just been some erotic creation of her imagination. All day she'd been trying to convince herself that that woman last night, wanton and eager, had been some stranger. Seeing him today, feeling the response that clamoured in her blood, made the truth hard to avoid. Like some drug-starved junkie she watched him from beneath the sweep of her lashes.

When had it happened? At what point had she fallen in love? She had never felt so insecure and bewildered in her life. This man had no use for her beyond the practical and possibly malicious reasons that had prompted him to wed her in the first place, she reminded herself. How was she going to cope with this? And not let him realise she loved him?

He shrugged and picked up a piece of driftwood, twisting it in his long, beautifully shaped fingers. 'As a matter of fact very little,' he said, throwing it carelessly over his shoulder. 'Four or five hours at the most.'

'Your island is beautiful, Morgan.' She had been watching his hands in a distracted fashion; only his sudden movement freed her from her fascination.

'Cay—that's the local way of referring to Sarisa and all the other small islands that make up the Bahamas.' He spelt it for her benefit, pronouncing it with a local twang as 'key'. 'Apart from the telephone and fax there aren't many concessions to the twentieth century here. If you miss the bright lights I can always take you over to Nassau.'

'I like it here,' she announced almost shyly.

'Are you saying you find my undiluted company sufficient? I'm flattered. Rachel hated it here.'

'I enjoy the solitude.' The sound of the other woman's name made her tense; was she expected to genuflect? she wondered bitterly. So Rachel had been here; strange, but she had somehow imagined he had never brought any other woman here. She had thought that this place at least was hers, that *he* would be hers. She inwardly chided herself for indulging in such wishful fantasies.

Of course Rachel had been here; she was the beloved wife, the dead saint who was the invulnerable rival... Who could fight a saint? Why should I want to? she asked herself angrily.

'Good; I'll let you have some as a special reward.'

Her temper made her feet sink viciously into the soft sand and her teeth were gritted. 'For services rendered?' she drawled bitterly. She didn't want to be worshipped, just treated with some respect.

He stopped in his tracks and swung her around to face him. 'I'd say service is its own reward in some circumstances. Last night was one of those occasions; you gave me what I asked for because you needed to,' he rasped. He gave a sound of impatience as she shook her head in denial. 'While we are here we can fight, or we can make love.'

'I think you're talking about sex,' she retorted fiercely. And how long would his present interest last? she wondered. She'd seen her mother's liaisons fade and die, liaisons between two strangers who had coincidentally shared intimacy. Beatrice had chosen to live that way out of preference, but the thought chilled Rosie.

'There's no need to make it sound unclean, Rosie. Sharing your needs with someone else, having them met, is nothing to feel ashamed of.'

It's not enough, she wanted to cry, but her lips stayed sealed. Always so sure of herself, Rosie felt pliable and fragile in his company; he would mould her to please him and then, when she was totally in tune with what he wanted, he would look for the next conquest. It was the nature of any predator and that was what Morgan was; beneath all the urbanity he was a hunter. And then she would be the hostess, the mother…never truly his lover.

'Are you self-conscious about last night?' he asked, a husky catch in his voice.

She spun around, silky hair flying. 'If you must know I'm disgusted that I fell for such a shallow package of sex appeal.' The words were filled with contempt. 'Perhaps I should have made allowances for the hereditary factor. I've watched my mother indulge her sexual hunger the same way, and with as little thought, as most people choose a new pair of shoes.'

And when the liaison was over she was able to walk away without regret, her heart intact, she added silently. If only I could, she thought despairingly, an expression of self-disgust contorting her finely drawn features. Her mother would have applauded sexual adventure, but to fall in love… Rosie had committed the cardinal sin.

'And you are so discerning, are you, Rosie?' he drawled, the tightness around his mouth the only external indicator of his reaction to her response. 'Who gave you the right to be so judgmental?'

'Me? That's rich coming from someone who has done nothing but sneer and pass judgement on me and my family. If you're talking about last night, that was an aberration—right now the idea of you touching me makes my skin crawl.' If I'm going to turn into some stupid, lovesick little slave at least I'll put up a fight, she vowed silently.

'It would take me five seconds to disprove that claim.'

The faint derisive smile that played about his lips made her want to resort to violence. Suddenly her anger faded and she felt deflated; what he said was true and they both knew it. 'I know you married me with the idea that I'd be some sort of breeding machine, Morgan, but a little restraint wouldn't come amiss. I agreed under pressure to become your wife, not the willing recipient of your sexual excesses.'

Her frigid, cutting response seemed to throw him off balance for a moment—but only a moment. Within seconds he'd recovered his usual confident manner. 'If you think any man could settle for duty, and clinical sex from a woman he'd shared a night of passion with...'

The cynical eyes narrowed and he made a disparaging sound in his throat. 'Whatever *excesses,*' he drawled cuttingly, 'I feel the need to indulge in, you apparently do too, if last night is anything to go by. You're my wife,' he reminded her arrogantly, as if that covered all her objections.

'Don't keep harping on about last night...it was a mistake.' She passed a hand over her forehead where fine beads of sweat stood out against her skin.

Her response didn't have sufficient force to provoke him this time and his eyes narrowed against the sun as he took in her flushed cheeks. 'Come along; you shouldn't be standing out here in the sun.'

'Thanks for the concern,' she muttered sarcastically, resenting the patronising tone he had adopted. She followed him; what choice was there? She'd already made her choice.

LUNCH WAS A DELICIOUS spicy seafood dish served with rice and salads, followed by a Key lime pie, which was mouth-watering enough to tempt even Rosie's appetite. After the first mouthful she abandoned the tempting idea of refusing sustenance and fading away before his eyes—the idea of seeing him wrung with remorse was highly attractive, but, she admitted, unrealistic; he'd be much more likely to force-feed her.

'Right, if anyone needs me I'll be in the study,' Morgan announced as he drained a glass of chilled Chardonnay.

Sally, who was busy trying to force more food on Rosie, looked at him with incredulous disapproval. 'I thought you'd be having an afternoon siesta,' she said, and her expression was so comical that if Rosie hadn't been busy combating her blushes she'd have laughed.

Bright sunshine filtering through the pale muslin drapes around the bed, dappled light playing across Morgan's skin, the sound of the fan…the smell of his body… The scene Sally's words had conjured up was so vivid that Rosie's heart began to beat a furious tattoo. She kept her eyes fixed on her interlocked fingers, lying demurely in her lap, anxious to conceal her inner turmoil. A hand on her shoulder made her start.

Morgan looked down at her with such a tender expression that her heart flipped, even though she knew this display was for Sally's benefit. 'Sally thinks I'm neglecting you, darling Rosie,' he drawled. 'After four p.m. I'm all yours, sweetheart…' The kiss was like a brand, not tender at all, and when Rosie emerged from it Sally was clucking like an approving hen. 'I'll teach you to dive if you like,' he offered, his eyes on her flushed cheeks and glowing eyes.

'I can't swim.'

'Then I shall teach you.'

She opened her mouth to protest but his finger on her lips effectively silenced her.

'It won't take long; you are *such* an enthusiastic pupil.' The grey eyes challenged her to dispute this but she remained tongue-tied.

Soon after he had gone she went upstairs to take a shower; it cooled her body but not her mind. Later, sitting on the wide, shady veranda dressed in loose, vividly patterned trousers and a white shirt that hinted at the faint golden glow that coloured her skin already, she tried to be as cool and composed as she looked.

She was glad of the company when Sally appeared bearing a tray of cool fruit juice. Smiling, Rosie accepted the drink.

'At least you don't crowd him like the other one,' Sally observed, lowering her ample frame onto the seat beside Rosie.

'Rachel, you mean?' she returned casually.

'You know about her, then.'

'A little,' she agreed, unwilling to reveal the avid curiosity that made her want to drag every snippet of information out of the woman. 'They were devoted…'

'Some might say that.' Sally swatted a fly with a wave of one plump arm. 'She certainly stuck to him like glue when they came here—only the once. It was too primitive, madam says. Later, when she dies in that plane crash, he comes back here. It was a bad time.' The dark eyes were sombre as she recalled the past. 'It's good to see him alive again.'

The beam she sent Rosie was an indication of her approval and Rosie smiled feebly in return, feeling a fake. Will-power had been responsible for any revitalisation Morgan had experienced, not her. Had he been different, then, in the days when he'd had a wife he adored?

A vicious stab of jealousy knifed through her. Had those incredible eyes shone with emotions other than cynicism? It was small consolation to know that he desired her; she was a body to him, to please him and bear him a child. When he had that child would he still want to retain even a tenuous link with her, or would he expel her from their lives altogether?

She listened to the elderly woman's story with only a small portion of her attention. 'You're drinking that punch awful fast,' Sally commented eventually.

'What? Oh, yes; it's delicious,' Rosie said with a smile. She emptied the last dregs from her glass and sucked a piece of fruit that had floated in the innocuous concoction. 'I suppose I'd better get a swimsuit for my lesson.' Her legs felt rather peculiar when she rose, and she swayed gently as she found her centre of gravity. 'Never do to keep the master waiting,' she declared cryptically.

When she returned downstairs Morgan was waiting in the hallway; he raised his brows as she arrived clad in a hip-skimming beach robe. 'Punctual and obedient, I'm pleased to see.'

Rosie was aware of the way his eyes were roving over her slightly clad body, and rather than being flustered she found it strangely exhilarating. She found herself experiencing the same sort of feeling that had made her choose an indecently brief bikini rather than a much more suitable one-piece.

'When it suits me,' she replied, meeting his stare head-on and not dropping her gaze. 'You were probably looking forward to dragging me by the scruff of the neck; I've noticed you lack subtlety,' she added, half to herself, as she strolled past his impassive figure. 'Aren't you coming?' She threw the words over her shoulder and padded away, her hips swaying in a provocative manner.

The sand was hot underfoot and she was glad of the shade of the palm under which Morgan paused. He peeled off his shorts, under which he wore a pair of swimming trunks. The upper body strength inherent in his deeply muscled shoulders and chest was balanced perfectly by his long legs, powerful thighs and flat, sculpted belly. She only realised she was staring when his eyes intercepted her hungry gaze.

'Hadn't you better take that thing off?' His voice was a low, growling caress, deliciously rough; she mentally compared it to the rasp of his shadowy beard against her delicate skin.

A strange sensation was throbbing through her veins and all her inhibitions seemed reluctant to respond to her bidding. Her eyelids hot and heavy, she just stared back at him. Her gaze slid down his body once more, caressing the powerful lines, as emotions seethed inside her head. With a small sound of protest she tore her eyes away and pulled the simple wrap up over her head.

The journey his silver-grey eyes made over her body was slow, comprehensive, silently articulate. The tension in the air seemed to draw in around them; the atmosphere throbbed with unspoken words…feelings. How could cold eyes burn like that? she wondered. She gained a small internal victory and, freed from her trance, fled towards the water, heedless of her name being called.

The water was warm and her usual fear was absent; perhaps the greater fear Morgan represented had placed it into proportion. She ran and then waded in, thigh-deep, waist-deep and then deeper still. Her footing slipped; quite how she was never sure, but the water that filled her mouth and nose made her panic completely.

Morgan lifted her, kicking and struggling, clear of the foam, her head nestled against the curve of his shoulder. She began to cough and splutter.

'Were you trying to kill yourself?' he demanded, the harsh lines of his face indicating his fury. He caught hold of a hank of her saturated black hair and pulled her head backwards. 'You were never out of your depth; all you had to do was stand up!' he yelled, unmoved by the tears that competed with the seawater on her face.

He strode out of the surf and dumped her unceremoniously on the sand. Rosie pushed her hair back from her face; she felt sick, stupid and extremely sorry for herself. 'You wanted to teach me,' she reminded him bitterly. 'I didn't expect you to drown me.'

'Give me strength,' he breathed, squatting down on the sand beside her. 'You ran into the water as though all the hounds in hell were pursuing you. One minute you were there and the next...' A hand raked his long hair and his jaw tightened. His head bent closer and his expression suddenly changed. 'You've been drinking,' he accused.

Rosie regarded him indignantly. 'I have not,' she contradicted him firmly.

He caught hold of her chin. 'I can smell it,' he said flatly.

'I've had one glass of wine with my lunch and you start interrogating me as though I'm some sort of secret drinker. Married to you, I might well resort to such forms of escape. Who knows how I might react to severe pressure?' She closed her eyes; actually she felt sick, probably from all the water she'd swallowed.

'Drinking and swimming is a fairly lethal combination,' he lectured sternly, ignoring her words. 'Although in your case sinking seems more accurate.'

'Don't lecture me,' she retorted weakly. 'I've spent almost all afternoon with Sally... We talked, and I've had some of her fruit punch.'

'You have, have you?' His capricious and totally devastating smile chose that moment to emerge.

'Have I said something witty?' she enquired crossly.

'Did you have much of Sally's delicious punch?' he asked, still grinning.

'I don't recall; two or three glasses, I suppose.' His preoccupation with the subject seemed perverse but she was beginning to feel really ill by this point. She was ill seconds later—violently ill. To her amazement Morgan showed no disgust; he didn't show much sympathy either but he did hold her head in a competent and comforting manner, for which she was grateful.

'Better now?'

She nodded wearily, and shivered as he lowered her robe over her head.

'The main ingredient by a long way in Sally's punch is rum—one hundred per cent proof rum.'

Eyes wide, she stared at him in horror; she'd been drinking it like fruit juice. 'Are you serious?' she asked hoarsely.

'Three parts rum, one part fruit juices. Now all the swaying hips and come-hither burning looks make sense,' he observed drily.

'I did not…' she began, flushing—a wry look stopped her as she realised that was exactly what she had been doing.

'Rum really can gnaw away at those old inhibitions,' he drawled. 'One school of thought says your true personality emerges when inebriation takes over,' he added thoughtfully. 'You really do sizzle,' he told her, with a low, appreciative whistle. 'I still can hardly believe you've never slept with a man before; you have a very tactile, passionate nature.' His voice had dropped an octave and the deep rasp was abrasive to her frayed nerve-endings.

She hugged her knees to her chest and for the first time in years remembered one of her mother's boyfriends making a very unsubtle pass at her. She had reacted without the poise he had obviously expected from a seventeen-year-old, and when he had complained to Beatrice that she had scratched his face for no good reason she had told her mother what had occurred.

Beatrice had reacted with a philosophical shrug and had given the young man his marching orders, but she had made it clear to Rosie that no man did that sort of thing without some encouragement. Later she had realised that her mother had responded that way partly as a defence mechanism and partly because she had seen Rosie's maturity as a sign of her own ageing.

The damage had been done, though, and at crucial moments over the years she had recalled with sicking clarity the man's rough hands and panting breath. It had always made her hold back part of herself; she had made sure she never gave any man cause to doubt her signals.

'There was an incident…' she began quietly. 'It wasn't

actually anything serious, not rape or anything. I should have been able to defuse the situation without getting hysterical.'

Morgan looked at her hunched figure with an elusive expression in his eyes. 'Tell me about it,' he said very softly.

Rosie looked at him with a curious, unfocused expression and did just that. After she had finished she felt strangely released, light; apprehensively she looked towards him, suddenly amazed that after all these years it was Morgan she had chosen to confide in.

'Is that the first time you've ever told anyone?' he asked, unwinding his long legs from underneath himself. He expelled a pent-up breath when she nodded. 'I think you know that nothing you did or said could justify what that man—and I use the term loosely—tried to do.'

'Of course I do.' It was a surprise that he could sound so confident about this. And she felt suddenly happier hearing someone else say it.

'It's a mistake to bury things; they fester,' he said, grimly reflective, and she knew instinctively that he was speaking from experience. 'I'm amazed that a woman as vain and selfish as your mother obviously permitted, not to say encouraged a beautiful creature like you to become a permanent part of her entourage.'

'I'm not a scene-stealer,' she responded wryly. Staying in the background, never competing had become a way of life that she'd stopped analysing. He had called her beautiful… The glowing response was impossible to halt; she radiated pleasure like a cat sitting in the warmth.

'You believe that?' he said slowly, incredulity lifting his voice. He shook his head as she looked uncomprehendingly back at him. 'You and your sister really are poles apart, aren't you?' he observed huskily, and then, devastatingly, 'I should have married her.'

If he'd hit her it would have been easier to stand, but

this harsh rejection had to be asborbed invisibly. 'We both wish that. Whatever misplaced loyalty made me get involved initially, I wish with all my heart I never had.' At that moment she realised how irrevocably she had fallen in love; the hurt caused by his abrupt rejection was in direct proportion.

He looked at her squarely, his face distant and at its most dautingly autocratic. 'That about covers it, I think, but the fact remains that we are married, and you could even now be carrying my child. So perhaps we should draw comfort from the few pleasures we can both extract from this farce. Come on; you can sleep it off.'

He carried her in his arms across the sand as if she were a child, and didn't comment on the tears that dampened his skin; his expression remained grimly austere.

CHAPTER SEVEN

BY SUPPERTIME ROSIE FELT considerably better—a fact that Morgan, after one comprehensive glance at her face, deduced immediately.

'Sally's left us supper; you get ready and I'll dish up.'

'I'm not very hungry and I've got a headache.' She pulled the counterpane up under her chin and glared at him.

'Hangover,' he corrected her unsympathetically. 'You'll feel better after food.'

'You'd know, I suppose,' she snapped pettishly.

'In my wild and decadent youth I did experience the occasional hangover. Nowadays I'm a reformed character; it was only the Harley I found impossible to part with.'

'Were you wild?' she asked, unable to restrain her curiosity. His veneer of civilised urbanity was beautifully polished but always she sensed it was thin; here on his island it was even more apparent that there was something marvellously untamed about this man.

'According to my family, beyond the pale,' he responded drily. 'My disruptive influence got me expelled from several schools. You could say formal education and I didn't mix too well. I bummed around Europe and later on the States for several years in my late teens and early twenties. My time of anarchic self-indulgence,' he said with dry self-mockery.

'Then one day someone introduced me to computers...' He shrugged. 'I had found something to channel my disruptive energy into, and I outstripped the bright boys who had trodden a more conventional path,' he told her, his tone matter-of-fact and not at all self-congratulatory. 'I returned home expecting to be greeted like the prodigal son. What do they say about a prophet and his own land?' he said wryly, his lips curved in a cynical smile.

'They wanted me to be an office boy basically and work my way up to the top. The firm my grandfather had begun had diversified into computers, but their ideas were hopelessly out of date. The frustrations of the situation were intolerable; that's why I eventually returned to the States to set up on my own. Rachel liked the States. Marriage was meant to turn me into a sober citizen—the first one, that is.'

She waited for the reminder of Rachel to inflict its usual pain and tensed. 'Did it?' He had almost implied that it had been an arranged marriage; how did that fit in with the romance of the century?

'I don't think she thought so,' he said, his voice strangely flat. 'Don't take long,' he added, turning dismissively, and Rosie had the impression that he regretted his cryptic comment.

She puzzled over his words whilst she pulled on fresh clothes—nothing too elaborate; it would never do for him to assume that she was out to please him. The loose silk sleeveless top was green shot with gold lights and the equally unfitted trousers were black; with her gleaming jet hair hanging sleekly loose down her back, the effect was almost Oriental.

Morgan was busy in the prosaic task of setting the table when she entered the room. He lit the candles with a glowing taper and extinguished the flame with the tip of his thumb and forefinger. At that moment he noticed her silent figure. Was his action or her appearance responsible for the pain that flared momentarily in his eyes? she wondered.

With exaggerated courtesy he held a chair out for her.

'Wine?' His lips quivered at her expression of disgust. 'Mineral water, then. I won't be long.'

All through the meal he waited on her. The conversation was safe but that didn't relax her; in fact it had the opposite effect and her tension escalated.

'Shall I clear away?' she said as a silence descended over the table.

'Sit still; I have strict instructions from Sally that we aren't to touch a thing. She only left to give us our privacy; we're not conducting this honeymoon along lines she approves of.'

She withdrew her eyes from his open collar; her breath felt tight in her chest. 'I feel guilty misleading her like this,' she said in a troubled voice. She shifted restlessly in her seat; the loose outfit seemed inexplicably hot.

'Our motivations are no one's business but our own.'

'I didn't expect you to share my qualms; conscience is a concept you are a stranger to.'

His expression grew taut; irony darkened his smoky eyes. 'But it's much more comfortable being a selfish, manipulative bastard,' he said laconically. He rose, stretching his tall limbs with animal grace. He took hold of the back of her chair and she felt the hairs on her nape rise as a shiver ran down her spine. 'Isn't that what you think of me, darling Rosie?' he drawled.

'It sounds an accurate assessment,' she agreed, flinching as his fingers touched the silken tips of her hair.

'Our marriage makes Sally happy, so don't waste your anguish on her.'

'Our marriage is a lie,' she said, her voice low and fierce.

He jerked the chair backwards, away from the table. 'You started that particular lie. I think truth is an overrated commodity anyway; most people flinch from it. What's the real motiviation behind your standing in for your sister? All I've done is follow a set of circumstances you set in motion through to their logical conclusion...I think it's bedtime now, don't you?'

The silky words made her clasp the arms of her chair spasmodically, her knuckles turning white. She stood up, aware that her knees were shaking. 'I want...' The thread of her thoughts eluded her, his eyes were so fierce.

His fingers ran down the silky length of her hair and came to rest at her waist. 'I want to be inside you.' The words were almost a groan, ripped from his throat, and Rosie whimpered as her body reacted violently to this starkly needy statement. 'And you want me there; you could have fought hard to escape, my Rosie, but the truth is you didn't want to,' he accused.

Please don't let him know, she thought despairingly. His breath was hot against her neck as he gathered her unresisting form close, plastering them together, hip to hip. The aggressive thrust of his hips against her belly made her aware of the extent of his need, and, to her shame, she responded with dangerous eagerness to the urgent masculine arousal.

I should be denying his accusations, she told herself as, belatedly, she realised what she was doing. Pushing hard against the solid muscularity of his chest, she tried to break free, panting hard.

He looked into her face, his own hard, driven, his eyes filled by a passionate glaze that made him look almost blind. 'You knew I wanted you earlier; considering the amount we were both wearing, it couldn't have been more obvious. You seemed to find the fact quite stimulating at that point,' he recalled throatily.

'I was drunk,' she said, wishing she could forget the blatant seductiveness with which she had acted. He was right—she hadn't been able to tear her eyes away from him; she hadn't even tried. The freedom she had experienced made her strangely wistful. 'You condemned that man I told you about, playing the sensitive, understanding male, and yet here you are, trying to do the same thing,' she jeered.

He released her so swiftly that she almost fell over. 'That's a distortion of the facts and you know it,' he grated. 'Whatever inhibitions you may have had about sex, you sure as hell don't have any with me. You may hate me, despise me, but, darling, you want me. When you've come to terms with that, I'll be waiting in *our* bed. I have never felt the urge to force myself on any woman.

'You are fighting yourself, Rosie, not me. I'm not about to take the responsibility for your actions away from you.' He gave her a scornful look and turned on his heel, leaving her gaping after him.

She sank back into her chair. Part of his accusation was painfully true; she did want him…oh, how she wanted him…although at times she felt she hated him almost as much as she loved him. He was right, she thought bleakly, to be so sure of her physical surrender. Her resistance had been mere window-dressing, to help her accept her ultimate capitulation, and he had known it.

She did have a choice; there had always been choices. She needn't have married him; true, the alternative had been unattractive, but not impossible. At no point in their lovemaking had there been any suggestion of coercion. A shocking thought occurred to her; had all her decisions been influenced by her initially denied but nevertheless devastating attraction to Morgan? As much as he appeared to desire her, mentally and emotionally he would always be unobtainable.

She got up, her back straight, her decision reached. She couldn't deny the part of her nature that wanted to go to him, any more than a salmon could prevent itself from swimming against the current. Yet although he might have her body her soul she had to keep safe from him. If he ever realised…the humiliation would be too great a burden to bear.

When she pulled back the canopy drapes that hung around the bed she'd already discarded her clothes. Morgan was lying there, the bedclothes skimming his narrow hips. He was intimidatingly beautiful; her breath rasped in her throat, where a pulse violently beat, as she stared.

'Morgan...?' His still expression wasn't helping her.

A feral smile, dangerous and silky, curved his lips as he met her frantic eyes. 'Who else were you expecting?' His eyes were distracted from her face by the pearly sway of her breasts as she slid inside the curtains. A jagged sigh emerged from the confines of his chest and he reached out and buried his face between the soft mounds of warm, quivering flesh. He breathed her name and his arms, strong and hard, tightened around her ribcage.

Her fingers dipped with shuddering, voluptuous pleasure into his hair; it was thick, rich, like gold silk, and she burrowed deeper, tracing the strong outline of his skull.

'This is your decision.'

'Yes, Morgan,' she agreed huskily, not even caring that his eyes flared with arrogant satisfaction.

Am I really this willing wanton? she wondered. Then all further thought was submerged by an avalanche of sensation; liquid fire ran in her veins and a glorious weakness pervaded her limbs...

'I DID IT, I DID IT,' she screamed with delight as she stood up triumphantly. She splashed the waves, sending a shower of water over him. She had swum exactly three strokes, of an indeterminate variety, before sinking. Impulsively she hugged him, her arms sliding around his waist and her face pressed against his chest.

After a moment's blissful pleasure, in which she enjoyed the sound of his heartbeat and the warmth that emanated from his salty skin, she suddenly, awkwardly pulled away. Over the past couple of weeks she had instinctively quashed any overt displays of affection. Morgan would find them distasteful, she was sure. Apprehensively she met his eyes. To her amazement he looked perfectly at ease; neither disgust nor scorn was evident. He seemed genuinely amused by her enthusiasm.

'Naturally you did; you have a brilliant and very patient teacher.'

'You didn't seem so confident yesterday,' she retorted. 'How did you put it...? The buoyancy of brick?' She tilted her head on one side and wrinkled her nose.

'Delete patient,' he conceded with a grin. 'Come on, water baby, let's go and eat. I thought we'd take a trip this afternoon in the *Lady*.'

Her eyes lit up with unaffected pleasure. The weeks of sun had turned her skin to a healthy shade of glowing gold. Due to Morgan's vigilance, or 'nagging', as she termed it, she had not suffered any burning. She paused to wring the excess moisture from her hair as she followed him up the beach. She'd already spent a day sailing around the island on Morgan's sloop, *Pretty Lady,* and she'd loved every moment of it.

The feeling of freedom that skimming across the waves evoked was like nothing she'd ever experienced. It had been a marvellous day; Morgan had dropped the habitual edge of caution he usually adopted when dealing with her...that distance he had almost visibly put between them on many occasions...and had allowed his natural charisma and vitality to emerge. He'd watched her wide-eyed appreciation with an indulgent smile. Until, that was, she'd caught his hand and almost shyly thanked him for a wonderful day.

She sighed, sliding the tall figure beside her a wistful look. He'd looked at her hand with such a strange expression, she recalled, that self-consciously she'd dropped it. Enigmatic bordering on brusque had been his attitude for the rest of the day and she'd refrained from asking for a repeat trip.

Only under the cover of darkness did all the barriers around them disintegrate under the force of their mutual passion. After nights that drained her physically and emotionally she would wake up beside someone who treated her like a stranger—a stranger who belonged to him, but nonetheless essentially a stranger. The contrast was bewildering and depressing.

During their lovemaking he seemed engrossed with her to the point of obsession. Discovering new ways of pleasing her, exciting her appeared to provide him with constant satisfaction. In her turn Rosie relinquished any limits she might once have mentally set upon their lovemaking; whatever pleased him inevitably pleased her, and her husband was a highly imaginative man, she'd discovered.

They had almost reached the house when Rosie realised his eyes were on her, watching the way the tip of her tongue was tasting the salty residue that had dried on her lips. His expression was raw; it evoked the hot, sweet warmth that only he could make her feel. A mere look and she wanted him, she acknowledged. This was a desperate situation, she thought suddenly, feeling a sharp, intruding shaft of fear. She'd reached the point where she was almost begging for his affection.

He moved towards her as if he'd read the sudden alarm in her expression. 'Do you still think I'd harm you…?' he grated huskily.

'I…'

'Phone call from London for you, Mr Morgan.'

Morgan gave her a look of frustration and strode off in the direction of the house. Rosie stayed a little while in the garden, lost in her thoughts, before following him. She had rung her sister two days previously and Elizabeth's shocked reaction when she'd realised how far the substitution had gone had been volcanic.

Her concern had mainly manifested itself in telling Rosie how idiotic she'd been. Confronted with an outright demand to know why she'd done something that was criminally insane, Rosie had been unable to admit what Morgan's tactics had been. 'I love him,' she'd simply said.

The words had slid out unrehearsed; they had cut short the flow of abuse, but the real concern that had followed had been worse by far. Without actually saying it Elizabeth had managed to convey the opinion that her sister would have to give Morgan Urquart a very loose rein indeed: he wasn't at all the type of man who played happy families.

Depressed, Rosie had responded with arctic politeness to Morgan's overtures over dinner that night. Later he had made love to her with an almost mindless passion that had left its mark the following day. In the morning he had touched a faint bruise on her shoulder, a frown furrowing his brow, his expression oddly bleak.

'I forget sometimes how delicate you are,' he had said gruffly.

Uncertain, she had stared back at him. 'I think I gave as good as I got,' she'd retorted huskily, thinking of the responses he had wrung from her. Certainly Morgan had given her a unique insight into her own character.

That had been the only occasion he had made love to her in the daylight hours, and the exquisite tenderness he had shown her had made her weep.

He emerged from his study after an hour, by which time Rosie, at Sally's insistence, had started her meal. He stood watching her, his expression enigmatic. 'I have to go back to London.'

She had known that eventually this would happen, but the reminder of the company which meant so much to him was like a physical blow; she felt sick to the stomach. This was no true paradise but it was probably going to be the most of him she would ever have.

'That's a pity,' she said breezily. She'd die before she'd let him see how badly she wanted this special time to go on.

'Is it?'

'Holidays end,' she responded lightly, and the expression on his face showed it was not the reply he'd hoped for; Rosie, however, more concerned with concealing her own feelings, didn't notice.

'We'll leave in the morning, first thing.' Dismissal was evident in his voice and she felt her cool, indifferent mask slip snugly into place. At times over the past week she had been able to pretend that theirs was a normal honeymoon; right now she cursed herself for such blatantly ridiculous fantasising.

'I'm sure you're essential to the smooth running of the company.'

About to leave, he paused at her acrid little comment. 'You had to be dragged here against your will, or so you'd have me believe.' The interest in his eyes had quickened perceptibly.

'I was merely thinking how satisfactory for your ego it must be to be indispensable,' she responded, shifting uncomfortably beneath his probing stare. Why hadn't she bitten her unruly tongue harder? she chastised herself silently.

'I thought perhaps you were reluctant to leave.'

She gave a convincingly incredulous laugh. 'I had no idea you had such a sense of humour.' She shook back her hair with a provocatively languid movement. 'Actually it will be good to get back to civilisation; I'm not really into rustic seclusion. I also intend to follow up a particularly interesting offer of a job.'

'You've been in the job market a very short time to be inundated with offers,' he drawled, his eyes hard and alert.

'Some people,' she shot back, incensed by his patronising attitude, 'actually appreciate my talents.'

The heavy eyelids, half-closed, nonetheless revealed the glitter in his eyes. 'So do I, Rosie.'

She felt hot colour flood her face. 'Gunther has offered me a job of managing his new gallery,' she told him, her amber eyes flashing fire. I hope the offer still stands, she thought, recalling her firm refusal at the time; had he actually been serious? she wondered worriedly.

'No.'

This autocratic assertion focused her attention once more on his face. 'I beg your pardon?'

'My wife will not be working for Weiss.'

Her incredulous wrath increased. 'I don't recall asking your permission,' she yelled. 'What am I meant to do—lunch with the ladies and have manicures while you're out being the big, bold bread-winner?' She gave a hoot of derisive laughter. 'Get real, Morgan; on your own personal island you may have been able to have me at your beck and call, but once we're back in England I've no intention of dancing attendance on you.'

'I think you'll find the job is no longer available.' He watched her rising temper with a cool indifference which was intensely infuriating.

'In other words you'll see to it it's not. I don't think you'll find Gunther is so easy to intimidate. You don't know him very well, it seems to me.'

The eyes that flickered over her heated face were deadly. 'Possibly it's you who doesn't know me very well,' he suggested quietly. 'I feel sure Weiss will see the... impropriety of employing you against your husband's wishes.'

She stood up, trembling with temper. 'Marriage to you seems remarkably like a prison sentence. Why don't we call it quits right now?' she flung at him wildly; anything would be better than being married to a man she desperately loved, yet who felt nothing for her. 'You have your precious company to play with and none of the other little boys can interfere. I'm redundant.'

'You're forgetting the other part of the deal; I want an heir.'

Her colour faded completely at this reminder. 'That's no

good reason to bring children into the world,' she said, her breath coming in short, shallow gasps by this point. Confrontation with him was so incredibly draining. 'If you wanted children why didn't you have them with your precious Rachel?' She wished the words unsaid the instant she'd said them; she wished she had resisted the devil that had prompted this childish and spiteful outburst.

He breathed hard through his flared nostrils and a thin white line etched the contours of his sensually sculpted mouth. His eyes were quite frighteningly bleak; Rosie wanted to look away from the pain but found she couldn't.

'Rachel wanted children; I wanted to wait... Who knows, if I hadn't things might have turned out differently.'

'No one can predict the future, Morgan.' The protest was instinctive; what did he blame himself for? His next words answered her question and stunned her.

'If I hadn't married her, she'd be alive today.' His harsh words were loud in the silent room. 'Don't fall in love with me, Rosie; it could be injurious to your health.' The bitter irony of his words made her flinch. His fingers raked through his leonine mane and a grimace twisted his features. 'Elizabeth would have been so much better.'

Did he have any notion of how deep those words cut? she wondered pensively, staring ahead, her eyes unfocused.

Long after he had left Rosie sat pondering his words; the incomplete information had offered a tantalising insight but little of any substance. Ellie had obviously been right when she had said that Morgan would only ever love his first wife. He seemed to have taken all the blame for her death on his own shoulders, but if her information was accurate the plane crash that had killed her and several other passengers had been due to a mechanical defect.

Did he wish that he had died with her? Now that she had experienced love, Rosie could understand how hard life would be to face if one was deprived of the person one loved.

'Elizabeth would have been so much better.' What had his feelings actually been towards her twin? Was that part of the reason for the extent of his anger when he'd spotted the deception? Perhaps all along he'd chosen Elizabeth because she was the one who had attracted him.

Is it my sister and not Rachel I should be jealous of? she wondered poignantly. Worse still, did he suspect the true nature of her feelings? She was mortified at this thought; his previous warning could have meant that. Misery swamped her and if there had been anywhere to run to on the island she would have, but Morgan, she knew, would always find her.

Morgan spent the rest of the day in his study; he even, much to Sally's dismay, ate there. And even though Rosie lay, her ears straining, all night, he didn't come up to their bedroom until daylight.

LONDON, DESPITE it being summer, was cool after Sarisa; so was Morgan. Whatever warmth there had ever been in his manner had vanished completely; he was preoccupied with whatever business crisis had drawn him back to England. He hadn't even returned to the house with her; ensconced in the back of a chauffeur-driven limousine, he had been deep in conversation when she'd last seen him. Alone in her new home, she recalled his comment that she would have to sink or swim. Her well-being came fairly low on his list of priorities; that much was obvious.

Rosie summoned enough courage to ring her mother, who was mysterious in the extreme. No complaints there that her life had fallen apart without her daughter; in fact she sounded positively elated. She didn't even make any wisecracks about marriage in general—odder and odder, Rosie thought, puzzling over the conversation afterwards. Still, no doubt all would be revealed in time; she couldn't really muster any great interest just now.

'Will Mr Urquart be dining at home?' the housekeeper asked.

'It's possible he might make it,' she said evasively, unwilling to display her total ignorance on the subject. As it turned out, she changed for dinner and sat alone in the dining room to eat it. Was this the way it was to be? she wondered. Inside she rebelled against the prospect and decided she had to do something...anything about the situation.

Gunther wasn't at home but she left a message on his answering machine, knowing he would return her call when he could. Despite Morgan's stupid objections she had to have some escape from this environment or she'd go mad. Pampered inactivity was not to her taste.

Returning to the drawing room where a tray of coffee had been laid out, she was startled to find Morgan standing there, his head bent intently over her sketch-pad. Impetuously she stepped forward and snatched it out of his unresisting hand.

'It's private,' she snapped.

He regarded her consideringly. 'I thought you weren't artistic...'

'I'm not,' she said firmly.

'I'm no judge but I'd say those—' he nodded towards the book clutched in her hand '—are good.'

'You're right—you're no judge,' she said flatly. With the botanical sketches she'd made a record of some of the flora on Sarisa. It had been an indulgence; she'd never intended anyone to see them. She cursed the nostalgic pangs that had made her look at them this evening. 'I have no talent.'

'It sounds as though you have that on good authority,' he observed shrewdly. 'Do I detect the hand of the great lady?' he enquired drily.

Rosie compressed her lips and refused to reply. It was kinder to be brutal, Beatrice had told her daughter, and nowadays Rosie could agree, though she still thought eleven was a little young to dash anyone's hopes. She knew that what gifts she had were paltry beside her mother's, but she did like sketching flora, enjoying the perfect symmetry of nature. Nothing bold and beautiful, like her mother's paintings, but it pleased her.

It was private, though, and Morgan had violated that privacy. Staring at him antagonistically, she realised how tired and drawn he looked; the lines around his eyes seemed etched deeper and his mouth was taut and tense. She firmly quashed the pain around her heart.

'You have no right to go through my things.'

He slumped down into a chair. 'Is that coffee hot?'

'Probably,' she said.

When she stubbornly didn't move he poured a cup himself. 'Are you afraid of rejection? Is that why you hide your scribbles? Your upbringing really has done a hatchet job on your self-esteem.'

'I accept my limitations,' she returned haughtily. 'There is a difference. I'm not afraid of rejection.'

'I thought you had more backbone,' he said with an expression of disgust.

'Happily I don't give that—' she snapped her fingers '—for what you think.'

'How cosy; home to the adoring little wife,' he commented drily, his lips curling. 'Pity you didn't get all this rebellion out of your system in your adolescence.'

'I had nothing to rebel against—no restrictive home life, no fierce morality codes. If you wanted an adoring wife you should have married Ellie,' she spat back. 'One minute you're instructing me not to fall in love with you—' her tone made this idea a joke and his expression darkened '—and the next you're complaining because I'm not acting the concerned wifey.

'I didn't even know if you were coming home tonight, as you didn't have the common courtesy to use a telephone. In future you can keep me informed; I have better things to do than sit around in this mausoleum all evening,' she said, casually insulting his exquisite home.

'Are you quite finished?' His mood didn't look promising; his grey eyes were like the chill waters of a swirling river—one with very dangerous undercurrents.

Bosom heaving, eyes still stormy, she glared her reply.

'I do not relish being spoken to as if I were some sort of recalcitrant schoolboy by a little shrew. The way I see it you have nothing better to do than wait for me, and if that's what I want you to do you will,' he stated imperiously.

His bare-faced arrogance took her breath away. 'Are you willing to stake money on that?' she enquired with interest.

'Certainly; I am happy to gamble on sure things. Don't come the wounded, plucky little heroine with me, darling; you knew exactly what this marriage was about. I need you to act a part; frankly I don't give a damn if you like it or not.' A hint of weariness had crept into his voice and he eyed her with a cold animosity that hurt her, and even when she was released from the full glare of his eyes the pain didn't fade.

'I'm quite happy for you to have outside interests but you'll put my needs first. You seem to have neglected a talent that many would envy and more would enjoy. You have a fine eye for detail.

'I have a friend who spends half his life journeying to wild and wonderful places to discover new botanical specimens—orchids from the Andes this time. A publisher wants to produce a glossy coffee-table tome of his discoveries and Jake has decided he'd like sketches of the specimens rather than glossy photos. I could introduce you,' he offered in an offhand manner.

She ignored the spurt of excitement that this idea gave her and shook her head stubbornly. 'I can do without your help.'

His eyes narrowed with cold contempt. 'You have a

pampered, privileged lifestyle; some women might envy you.'

She refused to be influenced by the grey tinge to his usually healthy skin tone. So he was tired...he'd survive, she told herself, hardening her heart.

'So might lap-dogs. I think you were born in the wrong century,' she breathed incredulously. 'I've already contacted Gunther about the job...'

The sudden blaze of fury in his eyes made her words fade. He leapt to his feet with feline grace, all evidence of fatigue obliterated. He was in a towering and awesome rage, it seemed. Somewhere in the stunned depths of her mind she registered the fact that his reaction seemed out of proportion.

'You've seen him,' he said from between clenched teeth. 'I forbid it,' he added, the soft, quiet emphasis in his voice more deadly than any ranting could have been.

'Gunther's my friend...' she began in confusion.

'I'm aware of that,' he said scornfully. 'And I'm sure that once he realises you are no longer resisting your sensual nature he'll be delighted. Why couldn't *he* help you discover the fact that you're a sensual woman, Rosie?'

'You're talking like a jealous man—' she began, then broke off, her eyes slowly widening. Surely he couldn't...?

'I'm talking like a husband who doesn't want his wife's name bandied around, or the paternity of his child questioned,' he said blightingly, and she felt ridiculous for having entertained her earlier notion. 'Besides, I keep what is mine.'

Tears of anger and frustration blurred her vision; how could she have fallen for such a monster? 'I'm not yours and I never will be, and I'll not have my friends sanctioned or vetoed by you.' His mention of a child had made her stomach churn; the calendar had made alarming reading earlier that day... Too soon to tell, she had told herself, but deep inside she already knew and the knowledge brought with it wildly conflicting emotions.

'Bloody stubborn—' He made an expansive gesture, flinging his arms wide. 'Fine; find your own job, do your own thing. But remember that you're my wife.'

'You aren't giving me much opportunity to forget that,' she observed bitterly.

'And of course you'd like to.'

'Under the circumstances what answer do you expect?'

The erratic nerve in his cheek leapt as his eyes swept over her. 'I *expect* that you'll never offer me anything of your own volition.'

His bitterness made her angry; what right had he to sound bitter? 'You're a bully, Morgan; your ego is too vast to accept that I don't want you.'

'I lunched with your sister today.' The totally unexpected comment made her stare at him incredulously.

'Elizabeth? You couldn't have,' she replied faintly. 'She would have come to see me.'

'No doubt she will.'

Rosie's mind was in a whirl. 'Why would she come to see you?' she asked suspiciously.

'For the pleasure of my company?' he suggested with irritating flippancy.

'Leave my sister alone, Morgan. It's bad enough that you've ruined one of our lives...'

His features tightened into an austere mask of disdain. 'It was your sister who sought me out,' he said in a dangerous, flat voice devoid of all expression.

While she had been here alone, trying to come to terms with a new life, new home, he had been wining and dining her twin. A rage that was as instant as it was strong took her over. 'I hope you both had a delightful time,' she said, her teeth clenched hard. How many times had he pointed out that she was a poor substitute for her twin? Jealousy made her ache with impotent misery. 'And here I was beginning to feel sorry for you after such an exhausting day.'

'You know, when I came home tonight I had nothing on my mind except falling asleep with your warm, fragrant breasts as my pillow and waking up in exactly the same place.' He looked at her, eyes darkly scornful. 'I've gone off the idea completely,' he revealed sardonically. 'I want a real woman.'

The images his words had evoked were painfully clear, and his subsequent disgust and rejection were like a whiplash. 'What a relief,' she said stiffly. 'Try and keep in mind the fact that Elizabeth is a married woman.'

His lips tightened in distaste. 'I've invited the managing director and his assistant from Japan to dinner tomorrow so I'll require your services. I believe they are bringing their wives, or at least female companions. Tell the staff and they'll do all the actual work, but I wouldn't like to be accused of not consulting you. All you need to do is look decorative and keep your acid retorts to a minimum.'

'I'll consult my diary.' I have to get out before I cry, she decided stubbornly, biting her lips. She didn't even notice the taste of blood in her mouth.

CHAPTER EIGHT

THIS DINNER PARTY was going to be perfect if it killed her! Where Morgan had spent the previous night was a total mystery to her, and, she told herself firmly, she didn't care.

If only that were true. None of her worst moments had prepared her for the agony of loving him. Just as none of her best moments had prepared her for the joy.

The white dress displayed her new tan most advantageously. The dress, one she'd never worn, had been an impulse buy. It was classic Greek styling—plain, leaving one shoulder bare and moulded to her body like a loving extra skin. The split in the skirt ran up almost to her thigh and the cunning cut meant that tantalising glimpses of her legs were given as she moved.

She'd piled her hair high on her head in a simple knot, allowing tendrils to escape; the effect was one she wouldn't, a short time ago, have dared employ. Right now, however, she wanted to dent Morgan's indifference—just, she told herself, so she'd have the opportunity to tell him how little he meant to her—and her appearance was exactly what she had aimed for.

The doorbell rang as she was rearranging the already perfect table decorations and the sound made her start; her nerves were already jangling like over-tuned piano wires. Morgan wouldn't have rung; surely the guests couldn't have arrived a full hour too early? she thought, panic-stricken.

The butler, impassive, impressive, arrived to announce a

guest seeking madam. When madam heard who it was a dozen conflicting emotions zipped through her.

'You've shown him into the drawing room? Thank you,' she said. Then, with ill-concealed eagerness, she lifted her skirts and hurried there.

'Gunther!' she cried in welcome as she flung open the door. If she'd been in any state to appreciate it, his wide-eyed appreciation of the vision that appeared before him would have been gratifying. As it was she ran impetuously forward and caught his hands. 'You got my message?'

He frowned and returned the grip of her fingers. 'No, *Liebling,* I've been out of the country.' He looked unaccountably sheepish as he told her this. 'If I'd actually thought you'd go so far as to marry him, I wouldn't have gone,' he added, with a deep frown. 'It was a foolish thing to do, Rosie.'

She wanted to cry; this stern criticism came from a heart which held no malice, only concern. Biting her lip, she controlled the tremors. 'I think it's the backlash of being criminally sensible all of my life,' she said huskily.

'When Beatrice told me you'd actually married him, I was horrified.'

'You've seen Mother? She rang me; she was very odd,' she said vaguely.

'I know.' His eyes slid from hers. 'I was there.'

The significant tone in his voice made no sense to her. 'Were you?'

'I have come to tell you, Rosie, that your mother married me two days ago in Athens.'

The stunned silence had gone on an unconscionable amount of time, she realised. Pull yourself together, Rosie, she told herself, seeing that the poor man was on tenterhooks waiting for her response.

'Gunther, that's marvellous.' She gave a shuddering sigh and threw her arms around him. 'Good God, you're my stepfather,' she said halfway between laughter and tears. They both burst out laughing.

'I wanted to break it to you gently; I think Beatrice is probably planning something dramatic, and possibly public.' He gave a small shudder but smiled manfully. 'I slipped out; you are entertaining?'

'Not for a little time yet,' she assured him happily. 'Tell me, how did you do it after all this time? If you don't mind me asking,' she added hastily, hoping she hadn't been too blunt. She slid her arm companionably through his.

'I gave her an ultimatum: either she marry me or I disappear out of her life for ever.'

'Amazing,' she said, impressed.

'I should have done it years ago. But enough of me; what about you?' he asked soberly.

It all spilled out then. Her head on his shoulder, she told the story of the charade, and its consequences, from beginning to end. He muttered responses in the correct places and patted her head gently. 'I hate to say I told you so,' he said finally.

'But you will anyway; have you got a tissue? I've made a complete mess of my make-up.' Smiling wanly, she accepted the man-sized handkerchief. 'I doubt if I can stay,' she said, voicing this knowledge for the first time.

'Believe me, I know how you feel; I too have been there. We rarely fall in love with suitable people—it's human nature—but it seems a tragic waste.' His eyes were so concerned, the tears almost sprang afresh, but she took hold of herself. 'Is there no chance…?' he asked.

'Of him loving me?' She shook her head emphatically. His bear-like embrace was comforting and Rosie found herself thinking that her mother was a fortunate woman; she hoped that Beatrice would treat this man as well as he deserved. Still, Gunther knew the worst and the best about her impulsive, frustrating yet charming parent.

He took her by the arms. 'If I had had the guts to take

the goat by the horns—' the fact that this error didn't even make her lips quiver was a good indicator of Rosie's state of mind '—this might never have happened. I would have been there to sort things out. It would have been my right. You must come with me, Rosie—home with me… I can't bear to see you unhappy, *Liebling*.'

'Oh, Gunther,' she said, hugging him. If only she could… No; she had to sort out this mess on her own, she decided reluctantly.

The slow handclap made them both start. Rosie spun around to see her husband, his tall frame propped up in the doorway.

'How delightful; I almost apologised for intruding and then I realised.' A deadly smile curved his lips and his eyes shot daggers of pure steel. 'This is my house, that is my wife; possibly I shouldn't be the one to leave.'

He straightened up from his negligent pose and there was danger apparent in every taut line and flexed muscle in his body. Glancing to her right, Rosie saw that Gunther had seen this too, and he reacted in a typically stupid masculine fashion. He stepped forward, bristling with macho aggression. His fists were balled at his sides. To her dismay, she saw that Morgan's swagger was a taunt all by itself.

'I'll be only too happy to leave this house but Rosie goes with me.'

'I think you'll find you're mistaken.' Morgan was at his silkiest but his grim eyes were continuously weighing up the other man. He was hoping the situation would escalate to violence, she realised suddenly; probably they both were… 'If you get out of here with your skin I'd consider that a plus if I were you.'

To the victor the spoils? I think not! she thought, a wave of revitalising fury wiping away the cornered feeling that the atmosphere of imminent violence had induced. She spoke Morgan's name, and when they both ignored her, too caught up in the tense ambience, she said it again. This time when she spoke her voice was icily strident and he did hear her; they both did. Their startled expressions gave her the distinct impression that both men, engrossed in their confrontation, had almost forgotten of her existence.

'You're both behaving like schoolboys, only you're both capable of causing more harm. I'm sure it would be fascinating to find out which one of you could damage the other the most,' she observed sarcastically. 'I'll pass if you don't mind,' she added with distaste. 'Gunther, I'd like you to leave.' She raised her hand to still his protest. 'I'm quite capable of dealing with the situation alone.'

She turned her attention to Morgan. 'If anything *you* owe Gunther an apology for behaving like some sort of Neanderthal. In case you've forgotten you have two important clients arriving in approximately thirty minutes—although a black eye would be a conversation point...' she observed with sweet malice.

'Well said, Rosie; I always have admired your practicality, darling.'

'Elizabeth! What...?' Her sister had been standing slightly behind Morgan, an interested observer of the noisy confrontation. 'Why are you here?'

Elizabeth chose that moment to move forward and take centre stage—her favourite spot.

'Why, your husband invited me to dinner, darling,' she replied in the languid, unhurried manner that was so much her own. Dressed in a tight-fitting red dress, she looked svelte and sexy as she glided forward and patted Morgan with casual familiarity on his arm.

Rosie's eyes couldn't seem to move from the spectacle of the red nails outlined against the beautifully cut dark fabric. Probing the sensation that convulsed her, she identified jealousy of a variety she'd never suspected existed; the sheer ferocity of it was breathtaking.

'It's marvellous to see you, darling, but possibly you should make a quiet exit at this point,' Elizabeth observed, looking in Gunther's direction. 'Rosie has an instinct in these matters.'

'Are you sure, *Liebling...?*' Gunther addressed his question to Rosie.

'Positive,' she said firmly, because she could see that Morgan didn't find this form of address acceptable; the clue was in the audible grinding of his teeth and the bunching of his fists.

'I'll see you out.'

'If you hit him...' she began, her eyes narrowed.

Morgan's heat had cooled to icy fury; the transformation was somehow even more alarming. 'I won't harm a hair on your *friend's* head,' he assured her grimly. 'But we do have some things to discuss.'

She had to be satisfied with that; at least she had averted a brawl, she realised with relief, hoping she wasn't being premature.

Gunther's eyes shot her reassurance and her husband's sent a message that was not at all comforting.

'Well, Rosie, that's the men out of the way... I thought your husband was going to flip when he saw you two. He really is magnificent in a scary sort of way,' Elizabeth mused, her tongue flicking out to touch her reddened lips.

'I'm surprised you didn't marry him yourself,' Rosie snapped.

'God, don't you go all moody and jealous on me too,' her twin returned, eyeing Rosie's hostile expression with dismay. 'After that phone call I had to see you.'

'So much so, you saw Morgan yesterday but managed to avoid me.'

'Rosie, love, I happen to be a happily married woman.' She smoothed her skirt and lowered herself into a chair. 'I got you into this, and Bill agreed that I ought to straighten out any misunderstandings I helped create. Good God, Rosie, you'd never have even met him if I hadn't used every trick in the book,' she said huskily, her face full of concern. 'If I'd thought for one minute you'd turn all human and actually succumb…'

Rosie didn't feel like being placated. 'Very selfless of you,' she muttered.

'Don't be like that.' Her twin got up and took hold of her arm. She stiffened abruptly and looked searchingly into Rosie's face. 'My God, you're pregnant,' she said suddenly, with something approaching awe.

Rosie caught her breath. 'How did you know…? I hardly know myself,' she whispered.

Elizabeth gave a peal of delighted laughter and hugged her twin. 'Perhaps we're developing this intuition thing a bit late.' Her grip on Rosie's arm tightened. 'The fact I'm in a similar situation could have something to do with it.'

Rosie's eyes widened and she gave a shaky laugh. 'It's great…isn't it?' she said tremulously. It was—or it would be if only Morgan… Her revolving thoughts came to an abrupt halt. 'Sorry I…'

'Thought I was here to steal your man,' her twin supplied wryly. 'I'm not surprised it comes as a shock to you to realise that I have a conscience. I think Bill just brings out the best in me,' she confided. 'I take it Morgan doesn't know…'

'Don't say a word,' Rosie said sharply.

'I'd say you know your business best, but after seeing the big German hunk all over you…'

'Gunther has married Mother.'

Elizabeth whistled silently. 'The poor lamb; wouldn't it be a hoot if she got all maternal too, and all three of us…?'

Rosie gave a chuckle. 'It would be a disaster!' she contradicted her firmly.

'Won't Morgan feel a fool when you tell him?' Elizabeth looked amused at the prospect.

'Morgan never feels a fool, even when he is, and if you tell him I'll never speak to you again. He's a pigheaded, arrogant swine!'

'Talking of pigheaded...' Rosie's glare cut her short. 'It's your life,' she conceded pacifically. 'But I was under the impression you'd fallen for said arrogant swine.'

Rosie chewed her lip. 'That's something else you'd better keep to yourself,' she added sternly. Then she froze as she heard Morgan push the door open to enter the room, and hoped she could rely on her sister's discretion.

Morgan's grey eyes were cold and implacable when he looked at her; for Elizabeth, she saw indignantly, he had a smile that was eighteen-carat charm.

'It wasn't what it looked like...'

The laugh was harsh. 'Not the most original line.' His voice had the cutting edge of a lash. His eyes were cold, opaque and quite merciless. 'I don't think we should embarrass Elizabeth with our domestic squabbles.'

'Don't mind me, people; pretend I'm not here,' Elizabeth said happily. 'Actually I think I'll go and freshen up,' she added, pulling a compact from her bag and frowning at her perfect reflection. 'Just as I thought—a fright,' she murmured, making her excuses.

'You're not interested in anything I say, are you?' Rosie observed bitterly when they were alone. I haven't done anything wrong; why am I justifying myself? she wondered with angry frustration.

'I'm always interested in good fiction.' The cruel twist to his lips made her heart ache; they had never been so far apart, she thought bleakly. 'You gave me your word you wouldn't see Weiss.'

'I did no such thing,' she gasped. '*You* ordered me not to, which isn't the same thing at all.'

'You intend to be brazen about this, don't you? If I'd got here a little later I'd probably have found you in bed.'

'Don't be stupid.' His raging contempt made her determined not to explain anything to him; he was the most wilfully cruel and unjust person on the face of the earth and she hated him.

'I'm sure you're anxious to make comparisons,' he sneered. 'Tacky to use my house for your sordid assignations, though, don't you think?'

'I thought it was my home too—not that I've found much evidence to support that claim,' she stormed, hating him more with every awful accusation. 'You have a mind that belongs in the sewers, Morgan; just because you have morals the average alley cat would be ashamed of, don't judge me by the same measure.'

'Oh, sorry, Miss Morality,' he drawled savagely. 'Considering what I saw and heard with my own eyes and ears, all these protestations of innocence sound a little hollow. I have to admit you had me thinking I'd been totally wrong about you.' The self-derision in his voice made her wince.

'At least your prejudice is consistent,' she snapped. He had a nerve; she didn't even know where he'd spent last night, and certainly not with whom. The idea of him loving…touching anyone else was intolerable.

'I won't have my wife behaving like some slut.' His face looked as if it was carved from stone, icy contempt in every austere line of it. 'If I can't trust you here, possibly it might be better if you stayed with my mother in the country. We could do with some breathing space.'

'I find your mother almost as intolerable as you,' she replied shakily. 'I'm not some child to be shipped off when I don't toe the line. If you think we need breathing space after little more than two weeks of marriage, don't you think that's indicative of a certain incompatibility?' she said bitterly. This conversation was ripping her to shreds but she had a perverse desire to inflict further punishment on herself by stating the obvious.

'Your tactics are getting repetitive, darling,' she sneered. 'You admitted you sent Elizabeth's lover off to the other side of the Atlantic. I doubt she would be so well disposed towards you if she knew that part of the story. Gunther's less open to your manipulation, so you want to send me off to some rural backwater.'

'Gunther Weiss will not be your lover; no man will be except me.' He was holding his internal devils in check with considerable difficulty. Throttling her was probably high on his list of desirable activities at that moment. Strangely, however, Rosie felt no fear; why she was so confident that he would never hurt her, at least physically, she wasn't sure, but she was.

If that statement had been made by a man who loved her, held her in any affection at all, her reaction would have been quite different. 'You won't decide what I do now or ever. I'm not one of your bloody acquisitions.' With an expression of extreme frustration she picked up a crystal goblet and hurled it to the floor. The sound of it smashing had a sobering effect; the resultant pieces almost exactly mirrored the way she felt inside. 'I'm not afraid of you, Morgan, so you have no control over me.'

'Not for yourself possibly, but what about your prospective lover?' The curl of his lips sent a shudder down her spine; he looked totally implacable. 'He won't be safe,' he said flatly, and, looking into his eyes, she believed him. 'What sort of man is he anyway? He had the opportunity to make you his and he didn't take it.'

'He's everything you're not,' she spat, thinking that unfortunately it was all the things Morgan was that she needed. What a waste—a criminal waste…all this love and he didn't want it.

'If you see Gunther Weiss again you'll discover what sort of man I am.' The smile that curved his sensual lips was the smile of a predator. 'I have to get changed; have that mess cleared away. That set of glasses has survived one hundred and fifty years,' he commented blandly. 'I really will have to do something about your destructive impulses.'

Rosie looked at the jagged shards on the carpet and felt

sorry to have destroyed a thing of beauty. She was oddly composed now: Elizabeth returned and raised her brows at the physical evidence of their confrontation.

'I take it you didn't tell Morgan,' she observed with a sigh. She looked with anxiety at her twin's pale face. 'Go upstairs and repair the devastation,' she advised. 'Not just to your face either. If you give him a chance...talk...you might find things aren't so hopeless,' she cajoled.

'No!' Rosie cried.

'Honestly, you're as bad as he is!'

'I know you want me to be as happy as you are but it's impossible; the whole thing is. He didn't even come home last night.' The sympathy on her twin's face was too hard to bear. 'I'll go and repair my face,' she said huskily, and rushed out of the room.

She tried to hurry, all the time aware of the sound of Morgan's shower in the adjoining bathroom, but her fingers were trembling, making the task difficult. He reentered the room before she had time to leave it. She stood, a slender figure, poised for flight.

Morgan moved into the room with a total lack of self-consciousness. He carried a towel, which was looped around his neck, his skin was still damp from the shower, and here and there small rivulets of water still ran over his bronzed flesh, she noticed, her eyes tracing one errant point of moisture as it slid down the flat plane of his belly.

Her tongue felt thick in her dry mouth; she couldn't have spoken if she'd wanted to. His raw masculinity had an effect similar to that generated by a strong electrical storm; were her eyes filled with the same heavy longing that had invaded her limbs? she wondered. Could he see the hot, tell-tale surge of blood that prickled her skin?

A hot, warm emptiness existed where her stomach was meant to be and lower the ache was sweet and strong. He was as beautifully elemental as a storm at sea, each line of him unique and awesome; his skin had the lustre of old gold. A golden god.

Their eyes met, hers glittering and feverish, his slitted and fierce. He knew exactly what she was feeling; the flare of hot triumph said so more clearly than words could have done. She was held captive by his eyes just as securely as if her hands had been bound.

After a terrible struggle she managed to move, break the sensual spell that had frozen her to the spot. She didn't look at him, though if she had the expression that contorted his features would certainly have surprised her. For this time there was no triumph at her humiliation, just a depth of torture that she would have recognised only too well.

The dinner party was horrific; she felt listless and empty. She smiled in the right places, but it was Elizabeth who really shone; sensing her twin's mood, she sparkled even more than usual. She was all the things Morgan had wanted *her* to be, Rosie thought, watching Morgan look on with approval as Elizabeth charmed his clients. She could well imagine his feelings when one of the guests mistook her twin for Mrs Urquart. He played his part, of course, but she was painfully aware of the cold sarcasm that tinged so many of his remarks to her.

'Will you join me for a nightcap?' he enquired after the guests had left. When she saw it was Elizabeth, not herself he was looking at it was the final straw.

'I need my beauty sleep,' Elizabeth said, giving Rosie a hug. 'Especially now,' she murmured, with a significant look at her twin.

'My driver will take you back to the hotel,' Morgan offered. 'Next time you come over you must bring Bill.'

'I think I'll let Bill bring me,' she corrected him with a smile. She gave Rosie a second hug. 'Look after yourselves,' she hissed in her twin's ear.

Rosie blinked away the tears and nodded. In a strange

way she had never felt closer to her twin in her life and her departure was painful.

Morgan was pouring himself a large brandy when she returned from seeing Elizabeth to the door. He watched her broodingly through the swirling amber liquid.

'You must be pleased with yourself; that went well,' she commented, ignoring the glass he held out. He shrugged minimally and placed it on the polished surface of the table. 'And that's all that matters to you, isn't it, Morgan—the company? You even married me for it. And a greater sacrifice than that is difficult to conceive. But then you're only going to make minor adjustments, aren't you? It's me that has to turn myself into a performing dog.'

'What did you have before that was so precious? Your precious job…propping up the vanity of a selfish woman who appears to possess not even the most rudimentary maternal instincts? You were a tight, repressed little virgin, too afraid even to try to draw, let alone love a man. I don't think you've lost too much by our bargain.'

She flinched as each flint-tipped arrow struck home. 'I had my freedom,' she said quietly. And now I have a child, she realised, and no one is ever going to take him or her from me, she decided fiercely.

He went pale beneath his tan and spoke her name throatily. She ignored the husky entreaty in his voice; he had hurt her so much; how could she bear any more? He seemed to actually hate her…would he try and take the child from her completely? The horror of the rogue notion made her swallow a moan of distress as she fled from him.

SHE MUST HAVE DRIFTED OFF into a fitful slumber eventually. The shifting of the bed as a body slid in beside her half woke her. Fingers gently ran over the slope of her shoulder, up the calf of her leg, gentle, unalarming, soothing. She closed her eyes, enjoying the soft caress and the luxury of not having to think at all.

The sensation of lips, cool against her throat, made her eyes flicker sleepily open. With a deep sigh she sank her fingers into the luxuriant mass of hair that lay against his neck.

'You're awake,' he murmured, his voice a hoarse, seductive whisper against her skin.

'You shouldn't...' she began, then a low growl escaped from deep in her throat as his hands moved lower, beneath the waistband of the pyjamas she wore. 'Morgan, I...' She gasped frantically for air as his sensitive probing, the exquisite sensations he was evoking, made her writhe.

'That's it, angel, relax; you only open up for me like this—no one else.' The sensual rasp of his tantalising voice was a breath in the sensitive confines of her ear. 'You looked so distant tonight in your vestal-virgin robes, but I know just how warm the blood that runs in your veins is.' He kissed her eyelids, her neck; his tongue traced the valley between her heaving breasts. In his hands they swelled and ached until she cried out, in a fever of unbearable bliss.

The slow seduction of her senses was complete; the fact that he was dominating her was no longer a problem, it was a pleasure. She accepted the hot, warm thrust of his tongue with a small moan. Her hands slid over his skin and the feel of his body tensing and the wild groan that vibrated through him as she touched the throbbing evidence of his manhood sent fire coursing through her veins.

'You're so perfect,' she moaned, the tang of him on her tongue. She was unaware of how hard her body was shaking as her eyes drank him in, wide and sultry. As her hands and lips moved over him he was shaking too.

His body arched over her and she began to babble his name, the word a litany...a plea. He was trembling as his knee parted her thighs and at last she felt him, hot and strong and part of her. She wasn't willing to accept anything gentle and restrained tonight and this desire communicated itself to him; thus the passionate coupling became a prolonged, savage struggle to bind their bodies together.

He seemed as exhausted as she was as they lay together afterwards, legs entwined still, his body half over her, his head resting on the cushiony firmness of her breasts.

'I am the only one for you, Rosie; can't you see that?' The muffled words were murmured against her skin. Only semi-conscious, her response was to thrust her fingers deep into his hair, securing his position against her heart.

SHE AWOKE THE NEXT MORNING from a dreamless, deep sleep. Nonetheless the weariness of early pregnancy seemed unabated. Morgan was gone. Last night and her excursion into unreality slipped back into her head. She had fallen asleep cradling the man she loved, her body richly rewarded by their lovemaking. Waking up with only crumpled bedclothes to bear witness to the event made her doubt the credibility of her memory.

She had convinced herself in the sleepy aftermath last night that she'd tell him about the baby this morning. Now it seemed fortuitous that he wasn't here… Why, I'm not even sure myself that I really *am* pregnant, she thought, justifying her cowardice.

She stretched luxuriously and padded barefoot towards the bathroom. A drawer in Morgan's bureau lay half-open; several items had spilled out onto the floor. She bent and retrieved the miscellany of objects and pulled open the drawer to replace them: Her thoughts were not connected with the mundane task—until, that was, the item that lay on top of the neatly folded objects in the drawer met her eyes.

At first she thought it was Ellie, and then she noticed the differences, though the similarities were enough to confirm Morgan's mother's statement that Ellie was the spitting image of the dead Rachel. She stared at the laughing face in the silver frame; the woman had a carefree smile and hair in a golden bob, giving her an angelic look. It gave no clues. It was there, though, and she knew immediately that Morgan had hurriedly replaced it this morning after taking it from its hiding place.

Had he thought of her last night as his hands and lips had touched hers? As his body had filled her, pierced her very core, had the image he carried been of this dead woman? She shook her head in a fierce rejection of the notion, but now that it had materialised it wouldn't vanish. It could be true; it probably was. I always was a substitute, but this… she thought with a shudder.

Carefully she replaced the picture, her hands shaking. She had to get away; she felt like a trespasser in this house—Rachel's house—and it was draining away her vitality the way a sponge soaked up water.

After several frantic minutes of throwing clothes into bags she finally thought of the perfect retreat. She'd go to Sarisa. Morgan was obviously going to be too busy here to leave for some time, so she would be safe from him. She couldn't stand Gunther's sympathy, and besides, her mother wouldn't welcome her return at the moment, if ever.

The fact that the island was an impractical destination didn't enter her head. She needed time to adjust to the imminence of motherhood and the reality of loving someone who would never love her back. He will want the child but he doesn't want me, she told herself. I need time to make my own decisions without being pressured.

She was propping up the note she'd quickly scrawled him behind the ormolu clock in the drawing room when a vistor was announced. She was just about to deny her presence when Ellie entered, not prepared to be kept waiting in the hall.

'Sit down, won't you? Will you take coffee?' she said with ingrained politeness. She smiled her strained thanks to the waiting maid when Ellie languidly agreed. 'I'm waiting for a taxi actually,' she said as the girl made herself comfortable, crossing her stockinged legs and admiring the effect; she did have excellent legs but Rosie wasn't really an appreciative audience.

'I came to see how poor Morgan is, under the circumstances…'

'Circumstances?' Ellie's eyes were filled with a venomous animosity that Rosie, usually receptive to atmosphere, was oblivious to at that moment.

'The anniversary of poor Rachel's death.' A cat-like smile emerged as Rosie's colour receded dramatically.

'I had no idea,' she said, her chin remaining firm by sheer will-power; the other woman was deriving great pleasure from her distress and she wasn't about to fall apart just for her satisfaction.

So now she knew why Morgan had had a furtive, poignant look at the picture of his dead love. She could imagine him looking from the picture to her very dissimilar, sleeping features. Did he feel disgust, distaste? she wondered. Or was there guilt? Did he feel he had betrayed a memory? Even in the heat of passion he had never once mentioned love; the omission screamed at her every time she replayed their lovemaking, which she did often like some helpless addict. Any frail hope she might have had that one day he might suddenly evaporated.

'After she died, we were anxious for his sanity. He went to pieces; he was totally unapproachable, worked all night mostly.'

'I'm surprised you were old enough to recall,' Rosie said drily. 'Morgan is a very resilient man and he needs little sleep, so I've found.' She deliberately made this statement ambiguous and Ellie didn't like it one little bit, she saw with no small measure of satisfaction.

'After the other night I assumed he didn't make a habit of spending too much time acting the dutiful husband.'

At that moment the maid appeared with the coffee-tray. 'Your taxi is here, Mrs Urquart, and Mr Bellis has your bags. He asks whether you're quite sure you don't want to use the car.'

'Thank you, but no. I'll be there shortly,' Rosie said, pale but outwardly calm.

'A little trip?'

Rosie smiled non-committally and ignored the eager, brittle enquiry. 'The other night?' she said in a carefully blank voice. Why deny the child the pleasure of telling her what she had so obviously come to say? How could he have been completely unreasonable about Gunther when all along he had…? Her façade of calm almost deserted her as she tensed, awaiting the information the other girl was aching to impart.

'Didn't you notice he was gone, then?'

'Say what you have to say and go—or rather stay if you want, because, as you see, I'm going.' The anguished noted in her voice silenced the girl's mocking laughter.

'He was with me.' She waited for Rosie to react, but when the blank expression on her face didn't alter she continued, her expression petulantly vindictive. 'He realises what a mistake he's made.'

'That's for Morgan to tell me, not you; I doubt if he'd be too pleased to know you'd been here.' For the first time the younger girl looked off balance. She glanced almost furtively over her shoulder.

'I'm leaving now; feel free to finish you coffee,' Rosie said quietly. She left the room carefully, not looking left or right.

Inside she was dying. Last night had been so perfect for her and yet Morgan had already betrayed her. At least she felt vindicated in her decision to leave. Had she driven him away, she wondered bleakly, into that child-woman's arms? How could he?

This was the close of the most important chapter in her life. She had explained to Morgan in the note that she had left, how impossible it was for her to remain, and where she was going.

Making her fall so disastrously in love was the cruellest thing he could have done to her, she decided. Did hearts, once broken, ever stop seeping the steady flow of blood? she wondered. Would she ever feel whole again? Unconsciously her hand slid to her flat belly as her thoughts turned to the child—their child. When Morgan knew she would never escape. To live with him without love was an agony she felt incapable of facing.

NASSAU WAS HOT and incredibly humid, and Rosie felt almost ready to sit down and weep when it proved unexpectedly difficult to persuade anyone to sail her out to Sarisa; for a population that was normally casual in the extreme, everyone appeared extraordinarily busy, she thought with frustration as once again someone rushed past her without noticing her question.

But she was made of stern stuff so she blotted the perspiration from her brow and doggedly continued to seek a boat owner willing to ferry her. For the tenth time she heard the hysterical comments about the storm which everyone swore was approaching. It was difficult to believe when she raised her eyes to the cloudless blue sky. When she made a ridiculously high offer avarice replaced the fear in this sailor's eyes and he made an equally outrageous counter-demand. He looked frankly incredulous when she agreed without a second thought.

The journey out to Sarisa made her suspicions about the fictitious nature of this so-called storm seem well justified. The sea was like a millpond. She longed for a breeze as her clothes clung damply to her sweat-soaked skin.

Her ferryman dropped her off on the jetty and landed her with much clucking of his tongue. 'Sure you won't change your mind, lady?' he asked as the last of the suitcases were extracted from the deck.

She shook her head, immensely relieved to be here. She didn't bother to analyse the impulse that had driven her; she just felt instinctively that something here would act as a salve to her emotional wounds.

'No, thank you,' she replied firmly. 'Could you take the cases up to the house for me?' she asked. His response brought an angry frown to her brow.

He leapt back into the boat. 'No way, lady, I'm out of here; can't spend money at the bottom of the sea,' he said, patting his pocket where the wad of cash she'd given him lay.

Considering the very laid-back attitude most islanders had towards time in general, she was surprised that this one was so reluctant to tarry. He had kept glancing at his watch all the way here; he obviously had an appointment to keep, she decided, picking up two of her cases and leaving the other for someone to bring up later.

The track up to the house had a slight gradient and, suffering under the relentless bombardment of the sun, she soon discarded one of the cases. The whole place was eerily silent and she was surprised she didn't see a soul.

The door to the house wasn't just locked, it was boarded, as were the windows. With a rising sense of panic she called Sally's name. She called until her voice was hoarse, but to no avail. There must be a perfectly logical reason for the complete desertion of the area, she told herself firmly; the only problem is, I can't think of it.

She sat on top of her case and leaned her aching head in her hands. Where was everyone? What was she going to do? She pushed that question to one side; it was the one that might make her give in to the raging fear that was building up inside her.

She ran down to Sally's bungalow, her heart pounding; when she saw the same blank windows she bit her lip, barely able to control her spiralling terror. Her sanctuary had suddenly become a very sinister place.

Deep breathing overcame her hyperventilation. She had to get in somehow; walking around the building, she found a window that looked less secure than the others. Using a piece of wood as a lever, she wrenched off the nailed planks; they were less secure than the wooden shutters on the big house.

It was less difficult to quash her in-built abhorrence of breaking into someone else's house than she had imagined. Avoiding the jagged glass, she reached in and lifted the latch. A little contortion and she was inside the neat little bungalow.

Room to room everything was incredibly normal; there was no clue as to why everyone had vanished. She gave a mental shrug of bewilderment as she sat on the chintz sofa. This *Marie Celeste* atmosphere was bizarre, but she stayed as calm as she could and didn't explore the cluster of sinister explanations that crowded into her head.

Someone had to be somewhere on the island; she just had to find them. With a wistful smile she pulled Sally's squashed straw Panama onto her head, remembering Morgan's continual nagging for her to have respect for the sun.

She tramped along the beach, calling intermittently, and it wasn't until the wind whipped the hat off her head that she realised the weather had changed. She chased after it along the beach to retrieve it, but could only watch as it was whisked high above her head, to be lost eventually in the waves.

Belatedly she recalled the warning of a storm; the sea was churning in a very alarming fashion, quite different from its blue opacity earlier. She squinted up and saw that the sun had been obliterated by a sullen, dark cloud.

Suddenly, being out here on the beach, exposed to the elements, seemed a bad idea. Walking at first and then running, she retraced her steps. She had only covered half the distance when the battle to stay upright against the gusts of wind which roared along the shore slowed her pace until for every step forward she took one step back.

The sand stung her face and arms, like tiny glass shards. When she opened her mouth to feed her starving lungs it filled with sand; she lowered her head and tried to fight her way through the solid wall of wind, the force of which was awesomely strong.

She let out a small shriek as a stray piece of debris hit her on the side of her head. She fell to her knees, dry sobs shaking her body, but the urge for survival took over and, though it seemed impossible, she stood up again and moved doggedly forward.

CHAPTER NINE

FOR A HALLUCINATION he seemed remarkably solid; the shelter of his body afforded Rosie an opportunity to breathe more easily.

'I knew you'd come,' she said stupidly as Morgan's hands moved to cup her face. A spasm contorted his features as he noticed the trickle of blood that seeped from her hairline; whether it was due to anger or distress she couldn't distinguish. 'I hate you,' she added matter-of-factly. Anger, yes, definitely anger, she decided, meeting the head-on assault of his luminous eyes, which were narrowed against the elements.

'We'll discuss that shortly,' he assured her grimly. 'Can you walk?' he yelled, his voice rising to compete with the howling of the wind that flattened his hair to his skull.

'Naturally…' she began, but he wasn't listening; he was half pulling her, half guiding her across the beach. His body gave her scant protection from the buffeting but his determination managed to resurrect her own.

He only had to carry her the last hundred yards through the trees that lay in front of the house. Deposited on the ground and instructed to lie flat, she did just that; the roar of the storm was the most frightening thing she had ever heard in her life. Like the wind, the sound had a body, a substance, that defied description.

'Come on.' She allowed Morgan to pull her towards the steps that led down to the cellar; the padlocked door had been forced, she saw, and he pushed her inside. The sudden stillness after the sensory assault was bewildering.

She sat on the stone floor and watched him attempt to secure the door, his face strained as the effort cost him every ounce of strength he possessed. His powerful muscles bunched and strained. When she joined him and set her back against the wood, digging her heels into the ground, he nodded his approval but didn't break from the effort he was making.

She heard the bolt shoot home with profound relief. Slowly she sank to the floor where she was. But if she thought the storm was over one glance at Morgan's face told her otherwise. Laughter was ludicrously inappropriate under the circumstances and she could tell from Morgan's low growl of disbelief that he certainly felt no sympathy for her helpless outburst.

'You find this amusing?' he yelled, levering his long frame off the floor and looming over her. 'Pardon me if I don't share the joke. I still can't believe even *you* could behave with such criminal insanity. To maroon yourself in the path of a hurricane...'

'Hurricane...?' she mumbled, as if the word held little meaning for her. Do I look as awful as he does? she wondered hazily. The remains of the formal type of suit he normally wore to work were in tatters; one arm was gone completely and the shirt beneath was torn to shreds.

'The one that has meant evacuation for most of the islanders, the one that meant I had to buy a boat because no one was willing to risk their life bringing me out here to strangle my insane wife. They didn't have your sort of courage—the sort that is the result of incredible ignorance,' he said bitingly.

'I shouldn't have left you that note,' she said bitterly.

'Note? What bloody note? I got no note, just Ellie telling me that it would be better in the long run and looking like a smug little cat. Why you saw fit to confide your plans to her and not to me... I came home to find *her* there and not you.' His knuckles cracked as he punched his palm with his bunched fist.

'I thought that was what you wanted.' Bewildered, she scrabbled to her feet inelegantly. One shoe was gone, she noticed, and she kicked the other off; it hit one of the dusty wine crates stacked against the far wall.

'What the hell are you talking about, woman? At least you're trying to destroy Uncle Charlie's hoard instead of yourself...that's some improvement. Was it that bad with me?' he grated, running his fingers through his hair. His expression was so bitter that it made her stare.

'You know it was,' she responded throatily. 'I wasn't trying to destroy myself, Morgan; the only self-destructive thing I've ever done is agree to marry you. As for telling Ellie anything, why would I? The girl loathes me; I left her in the house when I left. She must have read the note—taken it.'

'I found no note,' he began.

'She took it; I knew she hated me but...'

'Why would Ellie go to that sort of trouble?' he said, his expression openly sceptical.

She glared at him. 'Because you raised her expectations when you slept with her,' she said bitterly.

'I did what?' he exclaimed.

His shock looked so real that she almost allowed herself to believe it was genuine. 'If you didn't get my note how did you know I'd be here?' she asked suddenly.

He gave a grim smile. 'My staff are very loyal and George Bellis just happened to overhear you booking your flight.'

'I suppose you told them to spy on me.' She jumped as an extra sound was added to the cacophany that they were both yelling over. 'What's that?' she asked, her eyes wide with fear.

'Just the rain. You're safe here, Rosie—or as safe as it's

possible to be. The foundations for this place are deep in the rock; the cellars were tunnelled out.' His soothing tone didn't last long. 'What possessed you to come out here with hurricane warnings being shrieked from every news stand?' he demanded. 'It was nothing short of lunacy,' he added hoarsely.

'I honestly didn't notice,' she admitted, feeling, in retrospect, extremely foolish, but also marvellously safe with Morgan here. He had saved her life; eventually she was going to have to thank him. 'I was preoccupied,' she confessed wearily. He had followed her out here; he'd dropped everything and hared after her... Surely that meant he cared...?

She looked at his face, trying to read it, but it was as dauntingly enigmatic as ever. Don't forget Ellie, she reminded herself, feeling her defences weakening.

'So I gather. What idiot actually brought you out here?'

'A greedy one; he's probably on his way to the bank right now,' she said bitterly. 'He did try to tell me, I suppose,' she admitted, 'but the weather was so calm, I just thought they meant...I wasn't really listening,' she admitted. No, she thought; she had only been listening to the strange homing instinct which had drawn her here.

'Where's Weiss? Is he meeting you out here?'

She bent and lifted the lid on a packing case and looked under it. 'Not there,' she chirped. 'I can't imagine where he's got to,' she added sarcastically.

'If you want him this badly you might as well have him.' His facial muscles were clenched in an expressionless mask, and the fine dust coating that clung to his skin emphasised the deep tramlines around his eyes and mouth. He looked like stone.

'You came here to tell me that?' He didn't even care enough to fight, she thought; she was too much trouble. Inside she was all pain. 'Very magnanimous, and I don't suppose it has anything to do with Ellie,' she sneered sarcastically.

'Bloody Ellie! Why the hell do you keep bringing her into it?' He turned and pressed his bunched fists into the solid stone wall. She could see the muscles in his back ripple as his body tensed; his head fell back as he extended his neck. 'You said you hated me.'

She went deathly pale and made a gesture of denial, but he was too immersed in his own private soul-baring to notice.

'Rachel did too…eventually. I gave her no choice but to run away because I was too stubborn to listen to her, too selfish to let her go. I was afraid that history was going to repeat itself.'

His eyes held dark torment when he turned to face her. 'When I realised you were going to land in the middle of a hurricane…' A twisted, strangled sound emerged from the depths of his chest. 'If I hadn't caught the next plane after you I'd never have got here in time,' he said huskily. 'The rest were being diverted to Miami.'

'I d-don't understand,' she stuttered. 'Why would Rachel run away? She loved you.' Her mind was in a whirl as she silently digested his compulsive revelations.

'At first she did, yes,' he agreed, and the haunted glow in his eyes was terrible to behold. 'I married her because it was flattering to be worshipped, and to please my family. I had never done anything they approved of; I was always the maverick.'

He gave a self-derisive sneer. 'It was the worst thing I could have done. The more she gave, the less I wanted to give. My fondness turned to irritation and eventually her possessiveness…repelled me,' he admitted. 'I felt as if she wanted to eat me alive. She seemed almost to want to live vicariously, through me. But emotionally I was a barren zone for her.

'When she finally saw how shaky our marriage was, she

wanted children; she begged me; she was so convinced they would bind us together. I wouldn't even give her that.' The bleakness in his voice was profound. 'I know I had all the right answers; I told her that children shouldn't be used to cement unstable foundations.'

Hearing her own thoughts being spoken out loud, but in a context she had never expected, made her stare at him, compassion shining in her eyes.

'The worst part is,' he continued, self-revulsion in his voice, 'I didn't really care when she looked elsewhere for affection—it was almost a relief—but when she asked for a divorce I refused. In my pure, bloody-minded arrogance, I saw it as a sort of defeat, and I'm almost congenitally incapable of admitting defeat. I expect I'd have capitulated eventually, but it was too late…'

Her eyes shone with emotion as his hoarse voice faded away. 'The plane crash.'

His eyes turned back to her and he nodded. 'She was with her lover; they were both killed.' His abrupt gesture stopped her instinctive move towards him. She lowered her eyelids over the sudden rush of tears, knowing he would reject them just as he was rejecting her.

'Morgan, it wasn't your fault.' Taking on board all these admissions was making her head spin.

'History provides ample proof that the human race is incapable of learning by its own mistakes,' he said heavily. 'And my behaviour seems to verify that. I married you for my own selfish reasons and I've made you desperate enough to pull a stunt like this. Take Weiss; have him.' The toneless offer was somewhat spoilt by his snarled addition. 'And if he hurts you I'll break every bone in his body.'

Rosie found this last remark a glint of sun in an otherwise black sky. 'Shouldn't you ask me first if I want him?' she enquired with dignity. 'Or if he wants me, for that matter,' she continued with some fervour.

'Of course he wants you,' he snapped, with the air of a man who was already regretting his moment of generosity. 'You don't.'

'I've said you can have what you want,' he said throatily; his expression suggested that he was close to being pushed too far, but she felt certain that, for better or worse, she had to make that push.

'You've said I can have Gunther; *I've* never said that's what I want.' She ran her hand down her face, feeling the same layer of grit on her skin that was on his.

His face had a ravaged look as he froze, his eyes glued to her face. 'Are you saying that you don't want him?'

'If I did it would be too bad: he's already married.'

His tension exploded as he mouthed a violent obscenity. 'You knew he was married?' he demanded. 'I suppose he promised you he'd divorce and you believed him,' he said with incredulous scorn. His red-rimmed eyes looked like burning, hollow holes in his face; his skin was stretched tight over his bones.

'You saved yourself for him,' he spat in disgust. 'I'll kill him. If he comes within sniffing distance I'll... How could you even think of wasting yourself on a man like that? I won't permit it...'

'My mother wouldn't like it if you killed Gunther.'

Her words penetrated the red mist he was struggling to see through. 'What the hell has your mother got to do with it?'

'She hates black, and if you force her to wear it she'll never forgive you.'

'What are you talking about?' The grip on her arms was not gentle but Rosie only smiled faintly.

'She thinks it makes her look sallow,' she explained helpfully.

His eyes smouldered as he shook her. 'What has your mother got to do with Gunther? No more smart answers, Rosie.'

His warning was quite unnecessary; she had already decided she had gone far enough. 'Gunther married my mother earlier this week. He's my stepfather.'

He let her go as if burnt. 'Is that true?' he asked hoarsely.

'I'd hardly lie about it, would I?'

'Why didn't you tell me the truth?' he exploded. 'Have you any idea what I felt when I walked in...?' He wiped a hand over his eyes as if to extinguish the vision.

'Why should I? You were happy enough to condemn me out of hand. You didn't want to listen...' Her words trailed off into a whisper; the power of his gaze was almost hypnotic. 'What's wrong, Morgan?' she asked, rallying her spirit. 'Are you disappointed I won't be so easy to get rid of?'

'Why did you run away, then, if there was no lover?'

Her eyes slid away from his altogether too alarming contemplation. 'I explained it in my letter,' she muttered. 'And that was before Ellie told me you'd spent the other night with her.' The sound of his laughter made her turn on him, her eyes flashing, fists clenched. 'I didn't find it all that amusing.'

'You believed her?' he said incredulously.

'Are you saying it's not true?' she challenged, examining his strong carved features for signs of deceit. She wanted so badly to believe it wasn't true that she was afraid she was hearing only what she wanted.

'She's a child,' he protested. 'I know you haven't any great opinion of my scruples, but—'

'It's news to me you have any.'

The grim look around his mouth lifted as he grinned at this dry comment. 'Rosie, I haven't slept with Ellie. I can't offer proof, so you'll have to take my word for it. I slept at the office that night. I've done so in the past, though for different reasons. I was showering and changing into a fresh shirt when my mother put in a typically ill-timed appearance the next morning. I've no doubt she put two and two together and shared the information. It seems Ellie is quite a little opportunist, and you were all too eager to believe the minx.'

'I don't recall you offering me any apologies for being wrong about Gunther.'

'Does that mean you believe me?'

She eyed him warily and nodded.

'But you were leaving me anyway...running away?'

'I explained in my letter,' she muttered, her eyes sliding away from his gaze.

'I didn't quite catch that.'

She swung away from him, her body hunched defensively. 'I explained it in my letter!' she yelled.

He took her by the shoulders and firmly turned her around. 'I didn't get the letter,' he reminded her—again.

The touch of his hands was a special sort of torture. She slowly raised her face and met his unrelenting stare with sad-eyed dignity. 'I needed time to think. I saw the photo of Rachel in your drawer. I couldn't bear to be a substitute—not for her.'

He looked savagely satisfied by her broken admission. 'I never said you were.'

'You didn't have to; I may not be a substitute for Rachel but I've always been a substitute. I'm not even a very convenient one; you've never made a secret of the fact that you would have preferred Elizabeth. Last night it was easy to see why...' The tender expression that softened his hard features made her voice slide away to nothing. 'You don't want me...' she accused faintly.

The body that she was suddenly crushed against said something quite different. The kiss left her tingling with a delicous and dangerous excitement. 'It wasn't Elizabeth I spent last night making love to, Rosie. Incidentally, your twin came to demand to know what the hell I was playing at, marrying her sister. She wasn't very easy to placate, I can tell you...in the end I settled for the truth.

'I do want you; I have almost from the moment I realised you were Rosie, stubborn, argumentative and bewitching. I told her I love you.'

She made a soft sound of disbelief in her throat and quivered as his hand ran down the side of her face. His thumb touched the corner of her mouth and stayed there. 'I was mad as hell when I realised I'd been outmanoeuvred by my grandfather. I decided that if I had to marry I was not going to get involved in some emotional maelstrom. My one taste of marriage had proved me ill equipped to make a success of it. Your sister seemed the perfect candidate for a so-called modern marriage.'

He gave a slight grimace of apology. 'I know it seems callous to you, but you have to believe me when I say I had no idea she had any qualms. I had hurt Rachel enough by marrying her without being in love; I didn't want anyone vulnerable. I got you.' The irony had given way to a sort of wonder that made her head spin; the sensation of being in a dream grew stronger.

Rosie watched his face with growing fascination. She let this understandable assessment of her twin's character stand unchallenged; she was eager to hear more.

'I was mad as hell about the game you'd both been playing,' he admitted. 'Against all logic I decided I was going to marry you. I kept telling myself it was just a form of punishment.'

'To punish us, and still get the company and your heir,' she agreed, still not able to believe this bewildering change in him.

'My time was a long way from running out at that point, Rosie. I know I made you believe otherwise, but I could still have got some willing female to go through with a paper ceremony for a generous handout.'

Rosie stared at him; this startling confession changed matters in some very essential way, she realised, only she was too confused to figure out how at that moment. 'The heir—Elizabeth didn't even mention that,' she recalled.

He looked a trifle sheepish. 'Actually, that was an invention for your benefit,' he admitted huskily. 'I didn't want our relationship to be a paper one. I tried to convince myself that I was marrying you for purely practical reasons, but Rosie, my love, who the hell could believe being married to you could ever be practical? You drove me to distraction from day one,' he growled. 'I wanted you so badly I could barely think straight.

'The very first time I saw you with Gunther, so relaxed and at ease, I wanted to ram my fist in his face. Marrying you is the most selfish thing I've done in my life. Hell, I didn't even have the guts to admit to myself how much I loved you. I didn't think I was capable of loving...

'I was young and selfish when I married Rachel; we were two totally incompatible people. She was everything my family approved of—so conventional... Running off with her lover was the only reckless thing she did in her entire life,' he said, with an expression of deep remorse. 'She knew I didn't love her. I never loved anyone in my God-forsaken life until I met you,' he said rawly.

She reached up and took his face in her hands. 'Say that again,' she demanded fiercely.

'Which part?'

'Don't come the innocent with me, Morgan; you know exactly which part.'

'I fought it, my darling, my one and only love,' he admitted huskily, and suddenly the barren, stormracked cellar was transformed into the most beautiful place on earth. 'I found myself locked in a marriage where the love was distributed unevenly once more, only this time the tables were turned. A form of retribution, wouldn't you say?

'You are so damned prickly, woman, but you can't deny that together we are something special. I can teach you to love me,' he told her with arrogant certainty, his bone-deep self-confidence rising to the surface; but she had seen his vulnerability and she could see beyond the surface now.

'What are you asking me exactly, Morgan?' Spring was blossoming in her heart where before there had been a stark, arctic winter.

'I'm asking you to start again, give us a chance.'

'It sounded more like an order than a request,' she observed drily. His fingers were turning the gold band on her finger as he rocked her against his pelvis, one hand firmly on her waist.

'When I found you gone I'd never felt so desperate about anything in my life. I just knew I had to get you back, give us a chance at starting again—or you your freedom.' He said the last from between clenched teeth.

'Would you have let me go, then?'

His eyes held the dark glint of an avenging angel. 'In theory possibly, in reality…' He shook his head and his grip became fierce. '"To have and to hold…"' he quoted throatily.

'You can't teach me to love you, Morgan,' she told him solemnly, and the way he shrank from her physically and mentally was appalling; the slumberous passion faded from his face and a sombre blackness replaced it. 'Because I aleady do, you idiot,' she cried swiftly, privately resolving never to use the new power she wielded so casually again.

He paused, looking deep into her glowing eyes, and heaved an enormous sigh. 'You little wretch,' he breathed. He looked a different man; the lines of strain seemed to have melted away before her eyes.

Gasping for breath as she emerged from the series of deep, drowning kisses that followed, she laid her cheek against the damp hardness of his chest. 'You seemed to hate me so much, I couldn't stand it. Everyone kept telling me how perfect Rachel was; I felt sure you were constantly comparing me with her.'

'You, my little wretch, are quite unique,' he told her

firmly. 'I was broken up after she died, but from guilt rather than any more elevated emotion. It was my first marriage that was virtually arranged: a nice girl, of suitable stock, to settle down with. I don't think I ever expected to fall in love, so there didn't seem much harm in it at the time. The problem was, I couldn't give her what she wanted, Rosie.

'This marriage, on the other hand, has never been one of convenience; the moment I met you I decided I was going to have you and to hell with the consequences. My family knew straight off I was besotted with you.'

'They did?' she said, startled at this information. 'How?'

'My mother asked me, and I told her.'

'It's a great pity you didn't tell me,' she said, almost purring as she snuggled up to him sinuously.

'You'd have run a mile.'

'I'm not running now.'

As he met her clear, glowing gaze the last traces of anxiety that lingered in his face faded, to be replaced by a conflagration of passion.

The storm outside was as nothing compared to the one that raged within that quiet, dusty cellar sealed off from the world…

THE DEVASTATION after the storm was staggering. They walked silently past several fallen trees and debris; unrecognisable items lay everywhere. The sea was grey and churning.

'It could have been a lot worse,' Morgan said philosophically. His vibrant gaze was on her head as he spoke. 'I think the most important things have been preserved.'

The sober expression faded down her face as she lifted her eyes. She slid her hand into his. 'Something made me head for Sarisa when there didn't seem anywhere else to go. I think it's because my memories of here are so very precious; it feels like home.'

'Trust you to head in the opposite direction to the rest

of the world,' he responded softly. 'You realise we're stranded here until the evacuees return, don't you?'

'What about the boat you came in on?'

'I didn't have time to make it secure, let alone put it anywhere safe to ride out the storm. The only thing on my mind was that the guys on the quay remembered a crazy lady who had headed out to Sarisa Cay. I should try the radio and let everyone know we're all right before they start writing our obituaries.'

She nodded silently in agreement; the thought of Sarisa, Morgan and solitude made her smile.

'Why the smile?'

'I have you all to myself. I keep pinching myself to make sure I'm not dreaming,' she said, directing her languorous smile at him.

'I can think of better ways to prove that.' The touch of his hand on her sweetly sensitive breast made her gasp. 'I knew you couldn't not love me and be so gloriously responsive to me,' he said, sweeping her masterfully into his arms.

'I thought it was the last thing you wanted; I was terrified that you'd realise.'

'I can't conceive of life without you, darling Rosie.' He made this shuddering confession with adoring eyes and she jumped. His frown was instant. 'What's wrong?'

'I was pinching myself,' she admitted pertly.

'Is that a hint?'

'It might be,' she agreed. His mouth was a whisper away and she extended her neck to accommodate him. 'Could we arrange a less painful signal, though? Or I'll be black and blue before nightfall.'

'I love your lack of subtlety,' he said, his mouth extinguishing her throaty laugh.

Finally she pulled away from him a little and faced him, her expression grave. 'Does it worry you that two people from families that are not exactly brimming over with sensitivity and emotions might have trouble giving their own children a normal type of home?' she asked, the intended casualness of the question transformed into tremulous enquiry as her heart pounded.

'You're not...?' he said with an arrested expression.

She flushed rosily. 'I don't think children should be used to paper over the cracks in a shaky marriage either; that's one of the reasons why I needed to think. Also I thought that once you had a child I'd be even less important to you.'

'You poor, stupid darling,' he said huskily, framing her face with his hands. His eyes were glowing with a tender pride that started an answering glow inside her, and any remaining doubts and fears dissolved.

'I'd like lots of children—all girls like their mother,' he announced thoughtfully. 'As two products of less than perfect matings we will teach our children the language of love; after all, it's all we need, isn't it? Like this old house, I think our foundations are rock-solid. A hurricane is a harsh test.'

Her reply shone fiercely enough to put the sun in the shade as she gazed up at him with melting eyes.